WAITING
FOR THE
RANCHER

The Runaway Bride
A Bride of Convenience
Almost a Bride

Orphan Train Series
An Awakened Heart: A Novella
With You Always
Together Forever
Searching for You

Beacons of Hope Series
Out of the Storm: A Novella
Love Unexpected
Hearts Made Whole
Undaunted Hope
Forever Safe
Never Forget

Hearts of Faith Collection
The Preacher's Bride
The Doctor's Lady
Rebellious Heart

Michigan Brides Collection
Unending Devotion
A Noble Groom
Captured by Love

Historical
Luther and Katharina
Newton & Polly

Knights of Brethren Series
Enamored
Entwined
Ensnared
Enriched
Enflamed
Entrusted

Fairest Maidens Series
Beholden
Beguiled
Besotted

Lost Princesses Series
Always: Prequel Novella
Evermore
Foremost
Hereafter

Noble Knights Series
The Vow: Prequel Novella
An Uncertain Choice
A Daring Sacrifice
For Love & Honor
A Loyal Heart
A Worthy Rebel

Waters of Time Series
Come Back to Me
Never Leave Me
Stay With Me
Wait for Me

HIGH COUNTRY RANCH SERIES

WAITING
FOR THE
RANCHER

JODY HEDLUND

NORTHERN LIGHTS PRESS

Waiting for the Rancher
Northern Lights Press
© 2024 by Jody Hedlund
Jody Hedlund Print Edition
ISBN: 979-8-9896277-0-7

Jody Hedlund www.jodyhedlund.com

Cover Design by Hannah Linder
Cover images from Shutterstock

"Can't believe she's really gonna marry a scallywag like you." Maverick Oakley punched his best friend's arm. "She must be desperate."

Sterling Noble straightened his black string bow tie. "What can I say? I'm irresistible."

Maverick stuck a finger into his own bow tie and loosened it. Even then it still felt like it was strangling him, just like it had since the moment he'd put it on.

They stood side by side in front of the bureau mirror in the room Sterling had always shared with his brothers. Maverick was an inch or so shorter than his friend's six feet three inches, and he had leaner facial features with a square jawline and more prominent chin. His hair was darker—almost black—compared to Sterling's lighter brown, and he had blue eyes while Sterling's were brown.

Other than that, they both had rugged, muscular frames that came from years of hard work on their families' bordering ranches. Their skin was weathered from the sun and wind of Colorado's high country. Although most of the time they had a layer of scruff on their jaws, today, on Sterling's wedding day, they were both clean shaven.

Sterling was staring at himself, his eyes wide and filled with trepidation.

Maverick gave his friend a nod. "Violet's real lucky. You're a good man, the best. She couldn't ask for anyone better."

Beneath his collar and tie, Sterling's Adam's apple rose then fell. "Hope I can make her happy the way she deserves."

"You will."

A light rap sounded on the door.

Sterling didn't move, continued to examine himself as if he were counting his flaws and all the ways he didn't measure up.

"Come in." Maverick took charge for his friend, guessing he'd be nervous on his wedding day too. Not that he was getting married anytime soon. He hadn't cared about women, not for months. Not since his pa had died. He actually hadn't cared a whole heap about anything. Even today, he was having a hard time mustering the appropriate enthusiasm.

The door opened, and Hazel stepped into the room. "You fellows ready?"

Sterling's kid sister had her hair done up in a fancy style, with what appeared to be little pearls woven throughout. She was wearing a silvery gown that shimmered in the spring sunshine that was pouring through the room's tall window.

Maverick wasn't used to seeing her all gussied up. Most days at work, she wore her sturdy corduroy skirts, tall leather boots, a duster coat over a simple blouse, and a hat with her hair tucked up out of sight.

Even though he'd seen her nearly every day since she'd taken the position of broodmare manager last autumn, he rarely got a view of her fair hair, blond like a light-colored sorrel.

With her forehead puckered, her bronze-colored eyes swung between him and Sterling. "What's wrong?"

"Nothin'." He answered for Sterling, clamping his friend on his shoulder and squeezing. "We were about to head downstairs."

Hazel didn't respond, the sure sign she didn't believe him. That was the thing about Hazel—she could read emotions in people and animals better than anyone. It's what made her so good with horses and why his pa had hired her.

Maverick stuck a finger into his collar again, that familiar strangling sensation returning. His pa wouldn't be at the wedding today because of him and his foolishness. His pa wouldn't be at any event ever again, big or little, important or not.

An ache swelled in Maverick's chest, and he drew in a quick breath to try to push it back down.

At his intake, Hazel's gaze softened. He hadn't told her what he was feeling, hadn't shared about the remorse that was turning into self-loathing, but he suspected she knew, almost as though she could visibly see his pain and understood why the day was hard for him.

Giving himself a hard mental shake, he grasped Sterling by the shoulder and began to guide him toward the door. "Let's go, big fella. Time to get hitched."

Sterling went along willingly. "Reckon you're right."

Hazel moved into the hallway and waved them ahead of her. Sterling took a step, but then paused in front of the door across the hall, where Violet was getting ready with her sister and mother.

She was perfect for Sterling in every way. He'd been crazy about her since the day her family had moved to Breckenridge and he'd first laid eyes on her a year ago.

The trouble was that Violet didn't adore Sterling to the same extent—at least, from what Maverick could tell. She was a real nice gal and all, but there were times when Maverick wasn't sure she was ready to settle down.

He'd been surprised when Sterling had proposed marriage to her a few months ago, especially since the two hadn't been courting all that long. But Maverick had supported Sterling the way any best friend would. In fact, he'd even helped Sterling with his proposal plans, the plans they'd made when they'd been younger and had dreamed up how they'd each propose to the woman they fell in love with.

Sterling had decided he would propose by taking his true love skiing to nearby Devil's Glen, have a romantic dinner in an old miner's cabin there, and then ask her to marry him during dessert.

Maverick had been the one to ski out to the cabin ahead of time. He'd set up everything, including table linens, candles, and pine boughs to freshen the scent. He'd even brought the meal the Nobles' family cook had made. Maverick had ensured that every detail was perfect.

The January day had been beautiful, and the conditions had been just right. Sterling had proposed to Violet the way he'd always planned. The problem was Sterling had taken Violet by surprise, and she'd turned him down. He'd come back from the monumental event crushed.

The next weekend, Violet had apologized to him and accepted the proposal. Course, Sterling loved her enough to put aside his disappointment and had given her the ring again.

Now with the coming of April, the big day had arrived.

Sterling hesitated in the hallway. Was he thinking of stopping and talking with Violet?

Maverick steered him away from the door. "Naw, you don't get to see her yet."

Sterling shuffled forward. "Just wanted to talk to her through the door and make sure she's all right."

"Everything's fine." Maverick gave him a shove. "Now c'mon."

Sterling nodded, as though trying to convince himself that everything really was fine. Then he started down the stairs, and Maverick trailed him with Hazel on his heels.

Family and friends were milling about in the entryway of the Nobles' sprawling ranch house. The double doors leading to the front parlor were open, revealing more guests waiting for the start of the ceremony.

In years past, Maverick's whole family would have been at a gathering like this. His pa and ma and five siblings. But today . . .

His gaze snagged on his twin sisters, Clementine and Clarabelle, who were seated on a settee just inside the parlor where they were chatting with Mrs. Noble. Besides himself, they were the only Oakleys at the wedding. And Clarabelle had almost stayed home because she hadn't wanted to leave Ma's bedside.

Ma's pale face and listless body flashed to the front of his mind. Not only had his foolishness cost Pa his life, but it was costing Ma hers too. She was dying of a broken heart, and with each passing day, she was only getting worse.

Sterling finished descending amidst warm congratulations, but Maverick paused near the bottom of the stairway and swallowed hard.

What was more, without Pa there, the family was falling apart, and it was all because of him.

Maybe he hadn't been directly responsible for all that had happened to cause the big rift between Ryder and Tanner, but if Pa had been there, he would have known what to do to make them see reason. In fact, his two younger brothers probably wouldn't have started fighting at all, not with Pa intervening and bringing about peace.

At a gentle hand on his shoulder, Maverick shifted to find Hazel on the step above him. Her warm gaze seemed to encourage him that everything would be all right.

But he knew the truth deep inside. Nothing would ever be all right again.

He pulled at his tie, loosening it another notch. Even then, his breathing turned shallow, and he couldn't seem to get enough air.

With franticness rising inside, he glanced around for an escape and locked in on the front door. He needed to step outside . . . for a few seconds.

He broke away from Hazel's hold and descended the last couple of steps. "Be right back." He tossed her what he hoped was a grateful look. "Need a fresh lungful."

She was peering at her mother, who was motioning at her to hurry. "Don't take too long. Everyone is waiting for the wedding to start."

He was already winding his way past the guests to the front door. Although he was tempted to remind Hazel he wasn't holding things up, that Violet and Sterling were the ones dallying, he bit back his comment and pushed out the door.

He stepped onto the wraparound porch that faced Bald Mountain and the range lining the eastern part of Summit County. The rocky peaks were covered in a thick layer of snow that the high-altitude sun was slowly beginning to melt away.

The pasture spreading out in front of the Nobles' house was still barren and brown with patches of snow piled in the shade of boulders or brush. Hints of green were beginning to make an appearance, but it would be another month before blue grama grass began to flourish again.

As he crossed the porch and started down the steps, he sucked in a deep breath of the cool air. The dampness of soil and the waft of cattle and manure filled his nostrils.

He wasn't ready for the wedding, wasn't ready to be around everyone, wasn't ready for going on with life as if everything was the same as it had always been when it had all changed.

He followed the flagstone path forward several feet.

Then he halted and inhaled again, his sights on the towering range ahead. If only he could be as strong and solid as the mountains, just like his pa. But he was all too often hotheaded and hasty.

Squaring his shoulders, he stuffed his hands into his trouser pockets. As he swept his gaze over the beauty of the wild mountain valley, the sadness in his chest spread into his limbs. Although he loved the high country, no one had loved it more than Pa.

For the past fourteen years since leaving their horse farm in Kentucky, Pa had done everything he could to build a new life for his family in Colorado. After years of hard work, Pa had finally begun to see the rewards of his efforts. The High Country Ranch—or High C Ranch, as it was called—had gained a reputation for having the best horses in the state, possibly even in the West.

Maverick gave a shake of his head, as if that could somehow shake away the melancholy. He couldn't make today about him and his sorrow and regrets. This was Sterling's special day, and he had to be there for his friend and not stand outside feeling sorry for himself.

He shifted to return inside, but at the sight of a woman in a cream-colored gown leaning against the side of the house, he paused. The dark hair and pale skin were all he needed to recognize Violet.

What was she doing outside?

She had a handkerchief out and was blotting the

corners of her eyes, almost as if she were crying. What was wrong? Was she having pre-wedding jitters?

An urgency prodded him. He couldn't let Sterling see his bride like this, outside, crying. It would only make him more nervous.

Maverick shot a glance toward the front door, then to the parlor window. He could take care of this without Sterling being any the wiser. He'd talk to Violet and encourage her to go in right away and proceed with the wedding.

He veered off the path and strode across the flat tufts of grass. The dampness muted his bootsteps so that he was almost upon Violet before she glimpsed him nearing.

She pushed away from the house and rapidly began to dry her cheeks. "Hi, Maverick."

He stopped a foot away from her.

She averted her face and continued to blot at her eyes. "What are you doing out here?"

With his hands still stuffed into his pockets, he gave a slight shrug. He couldn't very well admit that he'd been overcome with guilt over his pa and family. She didn't need to hear that today. "Came lookin' for you, darlin'." The words were out before he could stop them. "Wanted to make sure you're okay."

She lifted her eyes, which gave him full view of the angst clouding them. "I don't know what I'm doing."

"I do. You're gonna go in there and marry the man you love."

"But how do I know if I really love him?"

How could she not love Sterling? The fellow was one of the kindest and most giving men Maverick had ever known. "Listen—"

"What if I have feelings for someone else too?" She straightened and seemed to pull in a steadying breath.

"You're just nervous. That's all."

"No. It's not all." She blinked back more tears. "I haven't been as sure about Sterling as he's been about me."

Maverick's gut cinched. He was glad Sterling wasn't nearby to hear the confession. "Don't matter none. Sterling's got enough love for the both of you." That was the plain truth. Sterling had been a goner since the day he'd laid eyes on Violet.

"I don't want to hurt Sterling." She pressed a hand against the long row of covered buttons that ran up the front of her bodice until she reached the brooch at the neckline. "But I just don't think I'm ready for this."

This conversation wasn't going the way Maverick wanted, and he had to do something—anything—to assure Violet that Sterling was the right man for her. He scrambled to find a solution. Maybe he oughta pick her up and carry her inside.

Without giving himself—or her—a chance to protest, he bent and swept her up into his arms. "C'mon. I'm taking you back in."

As he situated her against his chest, she wrapped her arms around his neck. Her skirt was full and the layers of material cumbersome, forcing him to hold her closer to keep from dropping her. He rounded the house and headed back toward the front door.

Her arms tightened with each step, and she lifted her head so that her cheek brushed against his. "Please. We need to talk."

At the plea in her voice, he halted. He dropped his gaze to find that she was looking up at him with furrowed brows. She was such a pretty woman. Not that he was attracted to her, but that didn't mean he couldn't admit she had stunning features, with pale skin that made her eyes and hair all the more vibrant.

"You're a good man," she whispered.

"Course I am." He offered her what he hoped was an encouraging smile.

She studied his face, ending up at his mouth. "You have such a nice smile."

"So do you, darlin'." He let his smile widen, hoping he could cheer her up. "I'd sure love to see your pretty lips smile right about now."

Her eyes only welled with more tears. "Oh, Maverick."

"I said I wanna see your smile, not tears." He gentled his voice.

"I think I have feelings for you too." Her arms

tightened around his shoulders.

"Whoa, now." What was going on here?

Her gaze trailed his face again. "I've tried to ignore the feelings, but they just won't go away."

"Don't go saying things like that." He lowered his voice to a hiss. This was bad. Real bad. Worse than bad.

"You can't deny you've been feeling things for me too." Her fingers at the back of his neck crept into his hair.

He had to fix things quick-like, before the situation went downhill even more. "Now darlin'—"

She rose up and pressed her lips to his, cutting him off. Her mouth was soft and her kiss filled with desperation. Her hands in his hair dragged him down, and at the same time, she deepened her kiss.

Maverick couldn't move. The shock of the moment paralyzed him. What was Violet doing? Why was she kissing him? And how could he help her see the error of her way? Help her realize the only man she oughta be kissing was Sterling?

At the banging of the front door and Sterling's shout, Maverick's heart plummeted. No doubt his friend was witnessing this whole interaction with Violet.

Maverick's muscles stiffened. He couldn't let Sterling find out the truth, that Violet had been the one to initiate the kiss. It would break his heart.

There was only one way to keep Sterling from

suspecting Violet had cheated on him. Maverick pressed into her. He'd take the blame for the kiss, act like it was his idea.

The instant he let his lips fuse with hers, he knew the plan was foolish, that it wouldn't work. That he couldn't kiss her in return, not for any reason. But before he could pull back, Sterling was grabbing his arm and wrenching Violet from him.

2

Maverick didn't have time to react or even think. In the next instant, a fist flew into his face, and knuckles slammed into his cheek.

The impact sent him stumbling backward with pain ricocheting through him.

Another fist pummeled into him, this one into his gut.

"You dirty, low-down dog!" Sterling's voice held a rage that Maverick had never heard there before.

Maverick finally glimpsed his friend coming at him with another fist. Maverick barely had time to duck before Sterling swung at him.

"Hold on!" Maverick held up his hands not only in self-defense but also to try to stop his friend.

Sterling's eyes contained the same rage as his voice. "You're trying to steal my woman!"

"No, it's not like that at all."

Sterling growled and then barreled toward Maverick, this time tackling him so that the two of them toppled over. Maverick hit the ground with enough force to drive the air from his lungs. Sterling landed on top of him but was still swinging his fists the whole time.

Maverick rolled out from underneath his friend. He'd wrestled enough livestock over the years that he was tough and could fend for himself.

Even so, he'd never been in a fight where he felt as though he might actually be in danger of losing his life. But with Sterling's expression twisted with deadly fury, a slight flicker of fear pulsed through Maverick.

"I was bringing Violet inside to you!"

Sterling grabbed him to keep him from getting away. "You were kissing her!"

Maverick wanted to deny his friend, to tell him that he had no desire for Violet. But it was better this way, for Sterling not to know about Violet's lapse in judgment, likely brought about because she was nervous.

Maverick scrambled in the damp grass to get away from Sterling. Even if he kept pretending that he'd been the one to start everything, it would still hurt Sterling. But stretching the truth wouldn't devastate him the same way Violet's betrayal would.

Sterling crawled after him, grabbing his legs and pulling him back.

"Fine!" Maverick shouted, ducking his head and

barely missing another fist to his face. "I got carried away. But it's all me, not Violet. She loves you and wants to marry you."

From the corner of his eye, he could see that the guests were spilling out of the house onto the porch and down the steps. Violet was now huddled against Hazel nearby, her face buried, her shoulders shaking with silent sobs.

Sterling pushed Maverick to the ground and planted the full weight of his body on Maverick. With his tie askew and streaks of dirt on his starched white shirt, Sterling set his jaw in a hard line. He pulled back his arm, his fist clenched, ready to throw another hit. Instead of rage, Sterling's eyes contained hatred, raw and unfiltered.

This time Maverick didn't fight to free himself. He laid his head back and stiffened in preparation for whatever further punishment Sterling wanted to dole out.

The hit came a second later, into Maverick's side. He could almost feel one of his ribs crack at the impact, and he closed his eyes to ward off the grunt of pain. More than that, he wanted to block out the hatred, something he'd never imagined he'd see in Sterling's eyes directed toward him.

As his friend's fist pounded into his gut again, Maverick didn't resist.

"No! Stop!" The shriek came from Violet. "Maverick isn't at fault. I am."

Sterling froze.

Maverick's gaze flew open and found Violet. She'd stepped toward them, but Hazel still had ahold of her arm. Tears streaked Violet's cheeks, and anguish lined her face. He could see that Violet intended to tell Sterling everything.

Maverick couldn't let that happen, although he didn't have a plan to prevent it.

"I'm not ready to get married." Her words filled the silence that was broken only by the wind chime on the front porch tinkling in the cool breeze.

Maverick could feel the fight beginning to ease from Sterling's body.

"I was already out here trying to decide how to tell you," she continued, "and Maverick saw me and was just trying to convince me to go through with it."

Sterling was shaking his head. "No. Maverick is always trying to steal the attention and sabotage things."

"No, I'm not—"

Sterling pressed his knee down hard into Maverick's gut, cutting him off. Then he turned pleading eyes upon Violet. "Please, don't say anything else. I promise we can work through this."

The tears were still rolling down her cheeks. "I can't go through with marrying you when I have feelings for Maverick too."

"He doesn't care about you like I do." Sterling's knee

dug into Maverick with bruising pain. "I'm the one who loves you, no matter what he's told you."

"Don't blame Maverick." Violet's voice turned pleading. "I started the kiss."

Sterling was shaking his head. "That's not true. Maverick did—"

"No! Sterling, listen to me." Violet's voice rose with a note of hysteria. "I can't marry you! Not when I don't know if I even love you."

Sterling grew absolutely still.

An ache formed in Maverick's chest—one that wasn't related to the beating. It was an ache for his friend at this ultimate rejection from the woman he loved and wanted to spend the rest of his life with.

"I'm sorry, Sterling." Violet spoke through broken sobs. "I should have told you sooner—"

"Please, Violet. Don't do this." Sterling's whisper was threaded with agony—an agony that tore at Maverick's heart.

Sniffling, she broke free from Hazel's grasp, picked up her skirts, and raced across the yard, away from the house in the direction of the nearest barn.

Sterling shoved Maverick one last time.

Maverick grabbed his friend's coat sleeve. "She didn't mean it—"

"Don't talk to me." Sterling jerked his arm free and tossed a contemptuous glance at Maverick—one containing the same hatred as moments ago, except more intense. As he stood and towered above Maverick, his gaze trailed after Violet.

Hazel made a move to follow Violet, but Sterling held out a hand to stop her. "I'll go talk to her."

Hazel nodded.

Already Violet's sister and mother were racing after the runaway bride. Sterling started forward but halted and glowered at Maverick. "You're an idiot, and I don't want to talk to you or see you ever again."

In the process of sitting up, Maverick felt Sterling's words almost as powerfully as a punch. He flopped back to the ground, a strange emptiness and pain radiating through his chest. He was tempted to defend himself and explain what had happened in greater detail, but he clamped his jaw closed. Even if Violet had already tried to take the blame, maybe Sterling still needed a scapegoat.

With a final contemptuous glare, Sterling jogged away.

Maverick hoped his friend would turn around and tell him he didn't really mean what he'd just said. But Sterling's shoulders and back remained stiff and unyielding.

The other guests were watching Sterling too ... except for Hazel. Her beautiful bronze eyes were trained upon Maverick. And they brimmed with disappointment.

With her hands on her hips and her head slightly

cocked, she watched him for a moment longer, as though attempting to understand what had driven him to his foolishness. Then with a shake of her head, she turned and walked away.

With four years' difference between his twenty-five years and her twenty-one, he'd been like another big brother in her life. He'd had a friendly and easy relationship with her, teasing and bantering like he did with his sisters.

The difference was that Hazel always had a sparkle in her eyes whenever she interacted with him—a sparkle that made him feel important, like he was her hero.

But here, now, he'd finally done something unforgivable. He'd proven to her that he wasn't anyone special. He was nothing more than a fool. He'd tried to help Sterling, but all he'd done was make matters worse . . . just like he'd done with his pa.

With an inner curse of self-loathing, he pushed himself up so that he was sitting.

Hazel was already near her parents and other siblings and had her back to him. He wanted her to turn around so he could smooth things over with a smile.

As if sensing his silent plea, she glanced at him. Her gaze was hard and accusing.

He blew out a tense breath and hung his head.

"Come on with you now." Clarabelle held out a hand to him. Clementine stood more stiffly, likely embarrassed by the turn of events.

While growing up, his twin sisters had been nearly impossible to tell apart in their appearances. At nineteen the two still looked very similar, with their pretty features, green eyes, and blond hair with hints of red.

But the differences were becoming more distinct. Clarabelle's skin was pale and unblemished compared to Clementine's, which had more freckles, especially sprinkled across her nose. Clementine also had a tiny scar on her chin from one of her many childhood mishaps.

While they were nearly the same outwardly, they were opposites in their personalities, with Clarabelle being quieter and more reserved, while Clementine was loud and outgoing. Clarabelle assisted at the school in Breckenridge but hoped someday to become a teacher. Clementine made candy and sold it at the general store but planned to have her own business eventually.

Course, over recent months, they'd both made many sacrifices to take care of Ma, neither one having all that much time to devote to their aspirations.

Maverick took Clarabelle's outstretched hand. Even though he didn't need the help in rising, he let Clarabelle drag him up to his feet.

"Let's go home," she said quietly as she eyed the other guests, who were now watching the three of them with decided hostility.

As he stood, Clementine slapped at his arm.

"Sometimes I don't know what to think of you, Maverick Oakley."

Sometimes he didn't know what to think of himself. But today, it wasn't hard to figure out. Sterling had summed it up well by calling him an idiot.

Today, he'd not only hurt and alienated his best friend, but he'd probably also severed his family's longstanding relationship with the Noble family. At the very least, the friendship between the two families would be even more strained than it had already become since Pa's death.

Had he also lost having Hazel as his friend and broodmare manager?

No doubt she'd never want to speak with him or see him again either. And for a reason he couldn't explain, that made everything that had happened even worse.

3

"You're not working for the Oakleys anymore."

At the harsh statement, Hazel paused in the dawn light just outside wide-open barn doors. She peered inside and found the source of the comment—Sterling—with a shovel in hand, mucking the stall closest to the haymow.

Even in the low lantern light, the dark circles under his eyes were noticeable, his expression haggard and his jawline hard.

In the two days since the failed wedding, he'd probably only slept a total of a few hours at the most. She'd heard him pacing both nights in his room. And he'd worked himself to utter exhaustion both days.

Now, at dawn, she'd hoped to find Alonzo to drive her over to the Oakleys' for work, but the old cowhand wasn't waiting for her with the wagon like he usually was. And she hadn't found him anywhere.

"Where's Alonzo?" She searched the shadows of the

barn, taking in the few dairy cows ready to be milked, the sow with her piglets in a penned off area, and a couple of barn cats perched in an open loft window.

"You're not going." Sterling's voice was firm, and he dug his shovel into the dirty hay as if the matter were finished.

She bristled under his tone. He was treating her like she was a child instead of a full-grown woman with a mind of her own. "I am going, Sterling. I like my job, and I don't intend to quit just because you've decided not to be friends with the Oakleys anymore."

In all the years of working for the Oakleys on their horse ranch, she'd never intentionally skipped a day of work until yesterday. She couldn't stay away today too.

From the moment she'd risen from the bed she shared with her sister Scarlet, she'd known she had to go. Yes, she was still mad at Maverick for the way he'd been holding and kissing Violet on Sterling's wedding day. She hated the cavalier way he'd made excuses for his womanizing, for the way he'd hurt and embarrassed Sterling, and for the shame he'd brought to their family.

Yet she had an important job at the Oakley horse farm as the broodmare manager, and she wasn't ready to give that up—not yet, and maybe not ever. She loved being in charge of the mares. It was her life, everything she'd ever dreamed of doing and more—tracking breeding cycles, overseeing gestation periods, assisting with all the foaling, and providing the newborn care. Not only did she thrive in her work, but the Oakleys needed her. Shoot, the mares needed her.

When she'd been younger, she'd helped at High C Ranch with the horses as a regular ranch hand. Then last summer, Mr. Oakley had decided his herds and breeding operations had grown too big for him to oversee. So he'd started looking to hire a manager who was organized and efficient and knew the horses well. She'd expected him to employ a veterinarian or maybe a cowboy with years of experience.

So when he'd approached her and asked her if she'd take the job, she'd been flustered, hadn't been sure if she was qualified. But she'd been thrilled and hadn't been able to say no when Mr. Oakley had insisted she was the one he wanted.

Oh sure, someday she planned to get married and have a family of her own. But at twenty-one she was still young and had time left before she'd have to settle down. Secretly, she hoped that someday her husband wouldn't be opposed to her continuing to work at the Oakley farm as the broodmare manager.

Whatever the case, she'd missed her time at the Oakleys' with the mares and the foals, and she was going back.

Sterling had stopped his shoveling to glare at her. "Don't you dare choose the Oakleys over me."

"You know I love you, Sterling." She gentled her tone. "I'm on your side through all of this." She hurt for him more than he knew. And she was so angry at Violet that she doubted their friendship could ever be repaired. But this wasn't about choosing sides. It was about losing the most important part of her life. And she couldn't give it up.

Besides, spring was the busiest time of the year for foaling. Six of the mares had already given birth, and she still had ten more to go throughout the rest of the spring and early into the summer. Tiny was due by the end of the week. The gentle mare needed her, and Hazel wasn't about to miss the birthing.

"I'll always be here for you." She wanted to cross to her oldest brother and give him a hug. He'd always been there for her too—had supported her taking the broodmare job when both Father and Mother had reservations. "But you're not in charge of my life."

He continued to glare.

She held his gaze and didn't waver. She wasn't nearly the spitfire Scarlet was, but she could be stubborn when she needed to be.

Finally his shoulders slumped, and he leaned heavily upon his shovel.

"I promise I'm just going to do my job. That's all. I don't plan to talk to Maverick—not any more than I absolutely have to." She may have once admired him. In fact, when she'd been younger, she'd always liked him, thought he was the handsomest cowboy she'd ever laid eyes on, loved his sweet charm, and adored his humor.

There had even been a time a few years ago when she'd entertained fanciful notions about trying to win him over and getting him to notice her as a woman and not just his best friend's little sister.

But she hadn't known what to do, and every effort she'd made to talk to him or spend time with him had seemed to miss the mark. Maverick had continued to treat her like one of his sisters and nothing more.

She'd eventually resigned herself to the fact that he'd never like her as much as she liked him. Over time, she'd done well with keeping her secret feelings for him stowed away. She'd been able to do her work without constantly battling her girlish attraction to him. Only once in a while had the rush of emotions slipped out and taken her by surprise.

The truth was, she was mostly over her infatuation with him. Now, after the way he'd betrayed Sterling, she felt nothing but animosity toward him—well, and sadness. And regret. And disappointment. And frustration.

Of course, she didn't blame Maverick entirely for all that had happened, even if Sterling did and refused to see all the ways Violet had contributed to the problem. Hazel had sensed Violet's confusion and hesitancy all spring.

In fact, just a couple of weeks ago Violet had brought up postponing the wedding, had admitted she wasn't sure if she was ready to get married. But since Violet was usually an emotional and indecisive person, Hazel hadn't taken the concern seriously—had instead encouraged Violet with how much Sterling loved her.

In hindsight, Hazel guessed she should have taken her friend's confusion to heart. Maybe she should have listened better. Maybe she should have told Sterling about Violet's hesitancies.

Regardless, what was done was done. And there wasn't any changing what had happened. After hiding in the barn for a short while and refusing to speak with Sterling, Violet had ridden home with her parents and sister. Sterling had gone to town yesterday to talk to her again and had learned that she'd left the high country and was traveling east with her sister and mother. Although Sterling had tried to discover where she was specifically going, apparently Violet had told her father not to tell anyone, especially not Sterling.

Sterling had come home more crushed. Even though he hadn't said so, it was clear that his relationship with Violet was over.

Hazel had loved her friendship with Violet and had been looking forward to having Violet as her sister-in-law. But now the young woman seemed like a stranger, and Hazel couldn't keep from wondering if she'd ever truly known her friend.

The friend she'd known wouldn't have let Maverick kiss her, certainly wouldn't have kissed him back . . .

Hazel's thoughts returned to the scene outside the house two days ago, the one in full view of the parlor window. When Maverick had come walking up the path carrying Violet, all the guests inside the house had grown quiet. None of them had even known Violet was outside. Not only had everyone been surprised to see her, but they'd been shocked to see Maverick holding her so intimately against his chest, their faces close, their expressions so intense.

Sterling had already stepped outside, and Hazel had been close on his heels when Maverick had stopped and kissed Violet. Or had Violet kissed him? Had Violet spoken the truth? That she'd been the one to initiate the kiss?

It had been difficult to tell from the front porch.

Either way, the kiss had been inappropriate. Even if Maverick hadn't started it, he could have avoided it or put an end to it almost immediately. But he'd kissed Violet back and had lingered for a few seconds, giving Sterling a full view of his disloyalty.

Not only had Hazel been mortified to see her friend and Maverick kissing, but she couldn't deny that she'd also been slightly hurt. Violet already had Sterling, who absolutely adored her, practically worshipped the ground she walked on. She hadn't needed Maverick too.

Not that Hazel had any claim to Maverick for herself. They were only friends. And it wasn't as if Violet had known about the old infatuation with Maverick. Hazel hadn't felt the need to talk about it since it wasn't important.

Regardless, Violet had been selfish to try to gain Maverick's affection in addition to Sterling's.

As Sterling bent his head and resumed his mucking of the stall, Hazel released a breath of frustration. Her brother had nothing to worry about. She'd never fall prey to Maverick's charm or good looks.

With a heavy heart, Hazel finally located Alonzo. His loyalty to their family ran deep, especially because Father had hired him to work the ranch when no one else would even consider hiring a cowboy who'd had one of his legs shot off during the War of Rebellion.

Although Alonzo hadn't protested her returning to work the same way Sterling had, at first he refused to hitch the wagon, telling her that he was too busy to take her. When she'd said that she would walk the two miles to High C Ranch, he shook his head and, a few minutes later, drove the team and wagon into the yard.

All the ride there, Alonzo's anger toward Maverick was clear in every twitch of his leathery face. As they entered through the front gate and started down the long dirt road that led to the house and barns, Hazel eagerly took in the horses grazing in the south pasture, the wide variety including Morgans, mustangs, Percherons, Clydesdales, and the new breed, the Colorado Oakley.

As with every time she gazed upon the dozen or so stately Oakleys, a sense of pride swelled within her, since she'd had a hand in their creation. They were a hardy horse—tall, muscular, and nimble-footed, intended to be able to withstand the harsher elements of the mountains. They'd also been bred to be steer-savvy and hard-working.

The new breed was proving to be everything they'd wanted and more. They were growing in popularity, and ranchers from all over the state were willing to pay a hefty price for one. In fact, several of the Oakley foals not yet born had already been purchased.

The horses disappeared from her view as the road began to wind through a stand of lodgepole pines. She drew in a breath of the fresh scent of damp spring soil, her blood finally seeming to come to life after the past few days of heartache.

When the team and wagon rumbled past the trees and into a clearing, the main house came into view, still made of the original logs from when the Oakleys had first settled the land. Smoke rose from a central stovepipe projecting from the roof, the gray wisps curling into the silent, motionless morning air.

The yard was deserted except for a scattering of

chickens pecking about in the dead grass. Beyond the house, the barns and corrals and small cabins for the ranch hands also seemed deserted. Likely the men were already out on the range with the cattle, driving them to areas where the grass wasn't chewed down to stubs.

Although the Oakleys focused on their horses and didn't have the large herds of cattle that her family had, they still kept a fair number of steers that needed pasture. April was usually hard, that in-between time when the feed stores from the winter were nearly gone and the fresh grasses hadn't grown back yet.

As Alonzo directed the team and wagon toward the mare barn, the first of three large structures, Hazel's heart began to beat at double the speed. Even though she'd only been absent from work for one day, she'd missed the mares. She knew each one by name, their mannerisms, their temperaments, their preferences, even their communication. And she liked to think they knew her too.

When the wagon came to a stop outside the double doors, she gave Alonzo's arm a squeeze. "Thank you for bringing me."

His back was hunched, and he rested his forearms on his thighs, his empty pantleg tucked up against the stub of his leg that had been amputated directly above his knee. Beneath the brim of his salt-stained Stetson, his stringy, greasy brown hair was tied back with a leather strip. His sun-browned face was covered in a thick beard and sideburns. As he settled his gaze upon her, his expression softened. "It's all right, girlie. I know you love the horses, that's all."

She offered him a smile, thankful he understood her need to be there in spite of all that had happened.

"I'll be back at dusk."

"I'll be ready." At least, she hoped so. She never could tell exactly when her mares would go into labor. Even when the signs were all there, birthings weren't predictable. Usually Alonzo didn't mind waiting for her and often came into the barn to assist her in any way he could.

But now . . . she had the feeling he wouldn't want to help and wouldn't want to stay a minute longer at High C Ranch than necessary.

If only she could put her fear of riding horses behind her. Then she wouldn't have to rely on him, especially to get to and from work. But in all her years of trying to make herself get back on a horse, she'd never been able to. At this point in her life, she'd nearly given up hope that she ever could.

As she climbed down and then waved goodbye to Alonzo, he fixed on something beyond her, his eyes narrowed into dangerous slits.

She only had to follow his gaze to the barn entrance to know why.

Maverick.

He was disheveled, his Stetson crooked, one sleeve of his flannel shirt rolled up and the other down, one of his denim trouser legs tucked into his boots and the other half out. His jaw and chin were unshaven and covered in a layer of scruff, and his eyes were dark and brooding, absent of the good-natured cheer that usually filled them. Also missing was his grin. Instead, his mouth was set into a tight line, almost as if he wasn't pleased to see her there.

Her pulse tripped with sudden unsteadiness. Had she been presumptuous in assuming her job would still be available? Maybe after all that had happened, Maverick was just as ready as Sterling to put distance between their families.

She braced herself for the worst. Would he tell her to leave?

"I'm surprised to see you here." His tone was laced with frustration. Or was it defeat?

Her heart stirred with compassion even though she didn't want it to. "Your pa hired me to manage the mares, and that's what I intend to keep doing."

He didn't respond, but his expression said it all—the haggard drop of his chin, the weariness in his eyes, the lines grooved into his forehead. He probably hadn't slept any more than Sterling had.

Even though he looked like he'd been run over by a herd of cattle, he still was the most handsome man she'd ever met. It really wasn't fair that no matter what he went through, he always had an appeal about him that made a woman want to rush to him, throw her arms around his shoulders, and kiss him.

Of course, she didn't want to rush to him like that. But she couldn't deny his magnetism—never had been able to. She just had to put it out of her mind and focus instead on what he'd done to Sterling and Violet—how he'd ruined Sterling's chances at happiness. She couldn't forget that.

"So you don't mind working with the marriage wrecker?" His question held a note of bitterness, as if he'd just read her mind.

She drew in a steadying breath. "I can do my job without having to interact with you. In fact, it would probably be best if we keep our distance."

He released a short humorless laugh. "Probably."

Guilt pricked her. Her words had been unkind. He didn't deserve to be ostracized and punished by everyone. "I'm sure everything will be all right eventually." She offered the olive branch of peace, or at least as much of it as she could.

He shrugged as if to say he didn't quite believe her but stepped aside and waved her through.

She gave a final nod to Alonzo. Then she pushed forward past Maverick into the barn, letting the warmth and scent of horseflesh greet her. Even though it was like walking into her home, she had the unsettled feeling that nothing would ever be the same again.

4

He was a wreck. He had been since he'd ridden away from Sterling's wedding.

Maverick slowed his gelding at the sight of Hazel in the horse corral, leading one of the new Oakley foals with the mama grazing a dozen feet away. All he wanted to do was go talk with Hazel and try to apologize, but her words from when she'd come in that morning hadn't stopped ringing in his head. *I can do my job without having to interact with you. In fact, it would probably be best if we keep our distance.*

All morning, he'd tried to stay out of her way, tried to keep his distance the way she wanted. He'd spent most of his time out in the south horse pasture with one of the ranch hands, examining the Clydesdale that had a lame foot.

After much prodding and poking, they'd discovered the horse had a foot abscess. Since the creature had been too lame to cross the distance to the barn, Maverick had used his knife to carve down through the hoof right then and there in the middle of the field. When he'd reached the soft sole and the abscess, he'd cut into it, and a thin spurt of pus had been followed by a steady trickle. He'd had to enlarge the drainage hole, and by the time he'd finished, the horse had been able to bear his weight on all feet.

Even so, they'd brought the Clydesdale back and now needed to soak the foot in a bucket of warm Epsom salts to not only clean the spot but to also keep the problem from reoccurring.

Now, as he led the creature toward the barn, he couldn't stop himself from watching Hazel as she interacted with the foal, petting and scratching its belly, ears, feet, and hind end. She was training it, getting it used to being handled, so that when it came time for haltering and tacking, it would be accustomed to the process.

Hazel straightened and arched her back, as though working out a kink. Her hair was tucked away under her battered black Stetson, and she was wearing her baggy duster coat.

As she took a step away from the foal, her gaze landed upon him and the Clydesdale trotting along behind him. She lifted a hand to wave, but then she must have remembered the conflict of the past weekend, and she quick-like brushed a loose strand of hair off her cheek instead.

Maverick's gut tightened in protest. Even though she'd only been there for half a day, he'd had enough of the strained interaction and tiptoeing around. He was gonna have to go over and have a good jawing about everything. That's all there was to it.

He tossed the Clydesdale's lead line to Ross, the cowhand riding with him. "Take him on in. I'll be there in a minute."

Without waiting for a reply, Maverick aimed his gelding toward Hazel and the corral. He could tell when she realized he was coming by the way she focused on the foal and began rubbing the creature again.

Even when he reached the corral, she kept her attention squarely on the foal and didn't glance his way. From the side, he got a view of her profile—her dainty pointed chin, the narrow stretch of her jaw, the delicate shape of her ear, the blond wisps of hair circling about her barren neck.

She looked so mature, so grown-up.

When had she stopped being that sweet little girl who'd followed Sterling and him around? It had been a while. In fact, he couldn't remember the last time she'd tagged along with them for anything.

He dismounted and leaned against the split rail post.

She still didn't look at him and instead scratched the

foal behind both ears.

Was this her way of telling him she intended to follow through on her declaration earlier not to interact with him? Well, he didn't like it one bit. Especially not with her. Not when she'd always looked up to him.

"Blast it all, Hazel." He couldn't keep the irritation from edging his voice.

She paused and straightened, turning a wide-eyed gaze upon him. In the bright midday sunlight, the bronze of her eyes had turned from brown to gold. A bucketload of uncertainty was etched into her features.

"Is this what you're aiming to do? Punish me by ignoring me every time I come near?"

"No." The word came out hastily. "I mean, yes." Her lashes fell, and she bit her lip as her cheeks flushed a soft shade of pink.

Had he ever seen her flushed before? If so, he couldn't remember it, and he would have remembered her looking like this . . . so sweet and fresh and . . . and what? Fascinating? Enticing?

As though realizing that her cheeks were turning color, she pressed her hands to them, then began to shed her duster, clearly trying to blame her condition on being hot rather than embarrassed.

He had half a mind to tease her like old times. But he stifled the banter, knowing he had to iron out the ruffles between them first.

She tossed her coat on the rail beside him, then stretched toward the foal. As she did so, her blouse and skirt hugged her figure—a very womanly figure with generous curves in all the right places.

Again, he paused to take in her profile, this time starting with her Stetson and making a trail from her perfect forehead, elegantly shaped cheeks and nose, pretty, pert lips, and down to her neckline and the swell of her bust showing. His gaze almost got stuck there, but he forced it to her slender ribs, to her waist, and then to her curved hips and backside.

When had Hazel turned into such a mighty fine-looking woman? Course, she'd been pretty at the wedding on Sunday. And she'd looked pretty plenty of other times.

But today, at this moment, there was something about her that was different. Something that blared all too loudly that she was off-limits, that she was someone he could never have, even if he wanted her. Which he didn't. Because, obviously, she was his best friend's little sister.

He and Sterling had long ago agreed they'd never cross a line and show interest in each other's younger sisters. It was part of the pact of honor and respect they'd developed. And it had been easy to abide by since their sisters had been far younger and treated them like older brothers.

He supposed he'd grown closer to Hazel over the past years that she'd been helping out with their horses. They both had the love of horses in common, and they'd worked together a lot, deciding upon the mares to breed and all that entailed. He'd also tried to be present for each of the foalings, even though Hazel was capable of handling it all by herself.

The plain truth was, he counted her as one of his closest friends. He'd already lost one friendship and didn't want to lose another.

With an inward sigh, Maverick gave himself a mental shake. He didn't want to do anything else to jeopardize his relationship with her, including taking notice of how womanly she was. The reason he was viewing her differently today was because she was acting differently by ignoring him instead of admiring him. That was all.

"C'mon now, Hazel. If you're gonna keep working here, you can't ignore me." He tried to focus on her face, but his gaze dropped again, this time to her slender arms, her dainty wrists, and her long fingers combing through the foal's mane.

She paused and glanced at him sideways, her eyes especially big and beautiful. "So if I ignore you, you'll fire me?"

At the worry in her expression, his immediate denial got stuck in his throat. Was she afraid, after everything that had happened, he wouldn't want her here? It wasn't true. He'd realized yesterday when she hadn't shown up just how much the ranch relied upon her for so many things.

"I'm sorry, Maverick." She straightened, and again her blouse hugged her body too tightly. "I don't want to lose my job. It's just that I promised Sterling I would come here and do my work and wouldn't talk to you any more than I have to."

So, Sterling hadn't wanted Hazel to come back, had tried to talk her out of it. The news shouldn't have surprised him. But it was harsh. And it told him all he needed to know—that Sterling really did hate him and probably wouldn't ever forgive him.

The despair he'd been trying to avoid shot through his chest with such force that he had to grip the rail tighter to keep from slamming his fist into something. He shifted his gaze to the Tenmile Range to the west just beyond their log home and the barns. The peaks rose with grandeur, the slopes still snow-covered in places.

He lived in the most beautiful place on earth, their river valley and their land surrounded on all sides by the wild mountains. He loved their ranch with a passion that none of his brothers had felt. And he loved the horses more than anyone else, except for maybe Hazel.

But after all that had happened with Sterling, Maverick had been ready to give it all up a dozen different times in order to go back and relive that day. In fact, he'd give it all up if he could have his friend back again. It meant nothing to him without the people he cared about.

"Maverick?" Hazel's voice was tentative.

He could sense what she was about to ask even before she formulated the words. And he wouldn't stop her. Even though he knew he deserved the punishment from Sterling, he wanted the chance to explain to someone all that had happened. Would Hazel listen? Or would she rush to judge him too?

She was quiet for a long moment, as if debating whether to bring up the painful subject. Finally she spoke in almost a whisper. "Why did you kiss Violet?"

He kept his focus on the rocky peaks, hoping to gain just a little bit of their strength. "It was a stupid, rash decision, one I'd do anything to change." After all, it hadn't saved Sterling any heartache. Maybe it had even made his pain worse.

"But why?" Hazel persisted. "Plenty of women fall right into your arms. So why choose her?"

Did plenty of women fall into his arms? He supposed some did. He was never without a partner at the local dances at Inman's Lodge. He always had women to flirt with after church services or at ice-skating and hockey games on Mill Pond. Whenever he went into town, he usually found one young gal or another to talk to. He supposed he could have picked one of them and settled down by now.

But none of them interested him all that much or for very long.

Hazel stood quietly beside the foal, waiting for his

answer, her fingers absently stroking the creature's forelock.

His action was indefensible, but he had to say something. "Would you believe me if I told you I kissed her because I was trying to take the blame for it and keep Sterling from knowing about Violet's doubts?"

Hazel cocked her head, studying him as though trying to see deep inside to the truth. "I want to believe you, Maverick. I really do. But you have to know how far-fetched your excuse sounds."

He expelled a sigh of defeat. "I know."

She left the foal and approached the fence. She stopped and placed her hands on the post on either side of his. "Was Violet telling the truth? Did she initiate the kiss?"

He let himself meet Hazel's gaze—her unassuming, trusting, clear gaze. "Would you believe me if I told you yes?"

Again she studied him, and this time her eyes were soft, almost kind. "You've never lied to me before. Why would you start now?"

A lump pushed up into his throat. Heaven almighty, he liked Hazel. She was the sweetest gal he'd ever met. "Thank you." His reply came out low and laden with emotion.

She shifted her hands so that they were on top of his, and she squeezed.

The ache in his throat pulsed higher. He wasn't a man given to blubbering, but he could feel the heat forming at the back of his eyes. The past two days had been pure torture, and now to have someone outside his family who was giving him even half an ear and not passing judgment? That was more than he could take.

He bent over and rested his head on the rail.

She kept her hands upon his, and somehow that simple comfort told him everything he needed to know— that she still was his friend and would listen to everything he had to say.

"I was feeling real bad about my pa not being there," he said quietly, not caring about the anguish in his voice. "And real bad Ma was too sick to come and that Ryder and Tanner weren't there either."

Hazel squeezed his hands again. "I guessed that was bothering you."

"It was getting to me something awful. So I stepped outside for a minute, and that's when I saw Violet crying by the side of the house."

"I didn't realize she'd gone out."

"Me either. Course, I went right over to see if she was all right. And she started going on about how she didn't know if she loved Sterling enough to marry him."

Hazel sighed. "I should say I'm surprised, but she'd shared her reservations with me on a couple occasions over the spring."

Maverick lifted his head and straightened. "She had reservations right from the start when she turned down his proposal that first time."

Hazel's head was still tilted in that endearing way she had about her when she was trying to figure something out. "I suppose there was a part of her that cared for Sterling and wanted to marry him. But she wasn't as ready as Sterling."

"I should've listened better to her. But I was just thinking about Sterling and how upset he was gonna be when he realized Violet was outside crying. So I scooped her up and started back to the house."

This time Hazel nodded, as if she finally understood.

"She told me she might have feelings for someone else." He forced himself to finish telling the whole sordid tale. "I didn't realize who she was talking about until she started to kiss me."

Hazel's eyes flashed with something. Was it anger? "No matter how confused Violet was, she shouldn't have been kissing another man while she was engaged and about to be married."

"I know." Maverick didn't understand how Violet could be so hurtful to Sterling. "The only thing I could think was that she'd been looking for a way out of the marriage and it was the only thing left for her to do."

"She should have talked to Sterling."

"Maybe she tried. You know how persuasive Sterling

can be when he wants something."

"True."

Maverick inhaled a deep breath, feeling suddenly lighter than he had since the wedding. "So you believe everything I've just told you?"

Hazel was still resting her hands on his. As if realizing it, she let go and stepped back. "I believe everything, Maverick. You were just trying to help Sterling by bringing Violet back up to the house. And maybe the kiss was her final desperate way to stop everything."

"Then you don't think I led her on?"

Hazel didn't respond right away. She gazed absently at the foal, a sturdy colt that was now nuzzling his mama, likely hungry after all the activity of the morning.

Maverick had been thinking through all his interactions with Violet over the past year and trying to figure out if he'd done anything to make her think he was interested in her. If he had, he hadn't meant to.

"In all honesty, Maverick," Hazel said, "you're a terrible flirt and sling around your smile and *darlin's* without any holding back."

"Darlin's?"

"*You okay, darlin'?*" She mimicked his tone. "*You want some help, darlin'? 'Cause I got plenty of help to give you.*"

He fought back a grin at hearing her reflection of his flirtation. "That bad, huh?"

"Worse."

He quickly sobered. "I never meant to flirt with Violet."

Hazel shrugged. "Sometimes I don't think you can help yourself."

Most of the time he was just trying to be friendly, but what if women took it the wrong way? "Blast," he whispered. "Why didn't Sterling say something?"

"Maybe he didn't want to admit to himself that Violet didn't love him back the way he loved her?"

Was Hazel right? Her theories made more sense than anything else. "How'd you get so smart?"

"Certainly not from hanging around you and Sterling." Her sarcastic statement was tempered by a tender smile.

A smile of his own broke free. There was just something about Hazel that had the power to comfort him and make him feel better. He wasn't sure what it was, but she had a calming, soothing, level-headed way that had always held her—and everyone around her—in good stead.

A gust of cold wind swept into the corral and swirled the dust. She crossed her arms and rubbed at her shirt sleeves as if to bring them warmth. The motion only seemed to accentuate her bosom, showing more of her curvy form and her creamy skin where her blouse curved low.

Had she ever worn the blouse before? Because for the love of all that was holy, it revealed miles of skin that led to her defined collarbones and her slender neck. Was her skin as smooth as it appeared?

As though she'd caught him staring at her chest or sensed the direction of his wayward thoughts, she lifted a hand and splayed it across the bare flesh.

He jerked his attention away, released the railing, and pivoted so that he was peering at the barns. What was wrong with him? And what was he doing?

She didn't move, stood frozen with her hand over her chest as though she was too shocked by his ogling to react.

He raised a hand and pinched the back of his neck, the tension swiftly rising there. He had to say something to excuse himself and apologize for his lust. But what could he say that wouldn't make things more awkward?

"Reckon I better head into the barn and check on that Clydesdale."

"Okay."

He didn't move, couldn't make his feet carry him away the way he should.

She didn't budge from where she was still standing with her hand over her chest.

He cleared his throat. "Thanks for letting me explain myself, Hazel."

"I'm glad you did." Her voice was soft.

He wanted to say so much more—wanted to tell her he appreciated that she'd come back to work, that she'd taken the time to listen to his side of the issues, that she'd tried to understand all of the dynamics at play, that she hadn't laid all the blame squarely at his feet. He appreciated all of that and more.

But at the moment, he needed to put a safe distance between them and clear his head. Without another word, he turned and forced himself to walk away.

5

"Tonight's the night."

Hazel rubbed her practiced hands over Tiny's udder. It was tight and engorged. The mare had also been running milk all day and had waxed up, the secretion on her teats another sign that she was foaling.

"You sure?" Maverick stood on the opposite side of Tiny in the large area of the barn they reserved for foaling. He was skimming her full abdomen. "She doesn't feel like she's dropped."

Hazel smoothed a hand across the mare's belly too, feeling the tautness and the slight movement of the unborn foal. "Usually I'm spot on."

"Not last time." Maverick's tone held a note of teasing.

"I've only been wrong twice this spring." She brought a comforting hand up to Tiny's chest, rubbing the mare affectionately. She was a mahogany bay Morgan but had been born more petite and delicate in appearance, earning her the name Tiny. "I have a pretty good record."

"I reckon it's all right."

She paused and straightened, glaring at Maverick over Tiny's withers.

He grinned back at her. He'd discarded his hat and coat, and now the last rays of the evening light coming in the high barn window glistened on his dark hair. Even messy from a full day of work, his hair was wavy and scattered over his head in a way that practically begged a woman to drag her fingers through it.

His eyes were equally enticing, the blue almost a violet color the same shade as the sky outside. And that grin? It was a killer just like always, making his handsome features come to life.

"Aw, c'mon now, Hazel." He drawled out his words, almost as if he were flirting with her. Almost. But she'd watched him flirt enough over the years to realize the difference between his teasing and flirting. For one, his grin was different. With her he always kept it friendly, without that devilish gleam. And for two, he never called her *darlin'* the way he did all the other women.

Just once, she wished he'd give her his devilish grin and call her *darlin'*. She was embarrassed to admit it, but she'd been filled with a strange, keen longing ever since earlier in the week, that first day she'd been back at work when he'd come out to the corral and told her the truth about Violet at the wedding.

She couldn't be sure, but she thought she'd caught him looking at her bosom. If he really had, he certainly hadn't done it for long. Even so, she'd felt a strange awareness of his presence ever since, as if somehow her body was attuned to his nearness and came more fully to life whenever he was around.

It was silly, really. He'd never looked at her as a woman, only as a sister, and he wouldn't start now. Not when everything was so tense between their families. Sterling had pressured her several more times during the week to stop working for the Oakleys. Even though Alonzo had continued to drive her over to High C Ranch every day, his glare was always in place as he pulled up in front of the horse barn.

Thankfully, Clarabelle and Clementine had welcomed her back to the ranch as easily as Maverick had, treating her with as much friendliness as always. And Mrs. Oakley was always welcoming. The dear woman had grown increasingly frail and rarely got out of bed anymore. She slept for long stretches, but whenever she was awake, she was as easy to talk to as ever.

The local doctor, Dr. Howell, hadn't been able to diagnose her ailment. The only conclusion he'd been able to draw was that she might have cancer.

Whatever the case, Hazel did her best to check in on Mrs. Oakley as often as possible. She'd always been like a second mother over the years, so sweet and kind and inviting. During the early years, she'd made the transition to the West more bearable, becoming like family to fill the empty spot created when they'd left all their family and friends behind.

Hazel had only been nine at the time her father had decided to move his law practice from Wisconsin to the West. Like many others, he'd been lured by the tales of gold. Since he'd always had a small farm, he'd wanted land in Summit County too.

At first they'd homesteaded the one hundred sixty acres allowed under the Homestead Act. But her father had eventually purchased much of the surrounding countryside, so that he'd become the largest cattle rancher in Summit County.

He'd also invested in several mining claims that hadn't netted him much in terms of gold. But just last year, silver and lead had been discovered in one of his mines, and now he'd turned his attention to the lucrative deposits, leaving the overseeing of the ranch to Sterling.

Maverick's brows rose. "You know you're the best at foaling in these parts. Ain't no one who can do it better than you."

She snorted and bent to finish her examination of Tiny. "You're just saying that because you know if I go home with Alonzo, you'll be stuck doing the foaling all by yourself."

Alonzo was still waiting outside the barn, and she didn't want to send him back to the ranch without her, not if Tiny wasn't really in labor. In the past, Maverick would have hitched a wagon and brought her home himself. But they both knew he couldn't do that tonight, maybe not ever again.

Yet if she stayed overnight and Tiny didn't go into labor, she'd risk angering Sterling all the more for lingering unnecessarily. And this week, and maybe for many weeks, they all were treading carefully around Sterling, trying not to do anything that might make him more upset.

"Maybe I should go." She tossed the words out halfheartedly.

"You know I can't come get you later. If I step foot on your ranch, Sterling's gonna shoot me full of lead—"

"He won't do that."

"I wouldn't put it past him."

"Deep in his heart he knows the truth . . ."

Maverick had stopped examining Tiny and was waiting for her to finish her thought, his broad shoulders and rugged muscular frame outlined in the evening light.

Her pulse gave a traitorous skip—one she wished she could control better. It was always hard to think straight with his blue eyes upon her, but she forced herself to ignore how good-looking he was just as she'd always done. "It'll take some time for Sterling to realize you're not to blame for Violet's rejection and to acknowledge that she wasn't ready."

"And what if he never realizes that?" Maverick's expression grew solemn, just as it did every time they talked about Sterling.

"He's smart. And someday he'll have to accept the truth."

"And what's that?"

"That Violet left him because she didn't love him and not because she loved you."

Maverick peered beyond her, clearly deep in thought.

She liked that about him, that he respected what she had to say, valued her opinion, and treated her like an equal even though she was a woman.

After several long seconds, his gaze flicked back to her. "You should stay. Send Alonzo home."

"Does that mean you agree I'm right about Tiny foaling tonight?"

"Fine. I'll cancel my trip to town."

Trip to town? Were the rumors true about him starting to court Winnie Sue Wheeler? She let her hand drift over Tiny's abdomen again. "If you want to go courting, don't let Tiny stop you."

"Courting?"

She moved toward Tiny's hind quarters and lifted the mare's tail. Sure enough, the mare gave little resistance, another sign the birthing was near.

"Who exactly am I courting this week?" Maverick's voice held a trace of humor.

She didn't find it funny and shot him a narrowed look. "A couple of the ranch hands were talking about you and Winnie Sue."

His brows rose. "What's wrong with Winnie Sue?"

She pressed her hands into her hips, not sure why his question needled her, but it did. "Are you?"

"Am I what?"

"Courting Winnie Sue?"

He opened his mouth to respond, then halted, his eyes lightening as he took in her expression. "You're jealous."

"What?" She could feel her cheeks flushing just like they had the other day when she'd been trying her best to ignore Maverick and he'd confronted her about it.

Why did he always have to be so direct? Why couldn't he be more subtle when he was teasing her?

"Of course I'm not jealous." She ducked lower, pretending to be busy with checking Tiny's thighs. "Why would I be?"

"Because you don't want me courting anyone."

This time she released what she hoped was a nonchalant snort. "I don't care who you court."

"Then why'd you bring it up?"

Why had she brought it up? If only she hadn't said anything.

"Admit it." His tone held a gloating note. "You want me all for yourself, darlin'."

She froze. He'd just called her *darlin'*. And no doubt if she glanced over at him, he'd be grinning one of his flirtatious grins.

Was Maverick Oakley, her longtime and forever girlhood infatuation, flirting with her?

Warmth spilled through her. She'd dreamed of such a day, when he'd no longer see her as a girl but would instead view her as a woman. Was that actually happening?

She hardly dared to breathe just in case she woke up and found that she'd only imagined their interaction.

She could feel Maverick watching her, waiting for her to banter back. But she wasn't an expert at flirting the way he was. In fact, she'd never gotten serious about any of the men who'd paid her attention, mainly because she'd always been too busy with her work.

Regardless, she had to say something, couldn't let awkward silence linger between them. "You're wrong." She tried to make her voice as nonchalant as his had been. "I don't want you all for myself, because I've got my eye on someone else."

The moment the fib slipped from her lips, she regretted it. What was she doing? She couldn't lie about being interested in another man. Not when the only one she'd ever liked was him.

Maverick straightened, and his easy grin faded. "Who?"

"Who?" Did he want her to name a name? A real person?

Maverick crossed his thick arms over his equally thick chest. "Yep. Who?"

Was he calling her bluff? She crossed her arms too and stared back.

His gaze dropped to her chest. Then it shot right back to her eyes. For a second, she glimpsed heat there—a heat that said he liked her body.

But just as quickly as the heat was there, he seemed to douse it with one blink. Before she knew it, his lips were curling up into a crooked grin.

Maybe she didn't need to be embarrassed after all. If he could so easily push aside his desire, then she'd do the same.

As two of the High C Ranch hands came in through the double doors on the far end of the barn, leading their mounts and teasing each other, she tried to remember their names. For a second she couldn't think of either, then when the taller of the two winked at her across the distance, she snapped her fingers. "Ross."

Maverick's gaze shifted to the newcomers, and his brow rose. "You're interested in Ross?"

From what she'd been able to tell from her infrequent interactions with the cowhand over the past year, he was a nice fellow—polite, respectful, and kind. He certainly couldn't compare to Maverick with his good looks. But there were qualities a whole lot more important than having a handsome face.

"I've had my eye on him." That wasn't entirely a lie because she had looked at him from time to time when he'd offered her a hand with the mares or foals.

Maverick watched Ross until he disappeared into a stall with his horse, then he turned his attention to Hazel, his forehead furrowed with obvious disbelief.

She needed to do more to convince Maverick. "Maybe you can give me some tips for how to get his attention."

"What kind of tips?"

"Oh, I don't know. Since you're the expert at flirting, maybe you can teach me everything you know."

Maverick's eyes widened. He opened his mouth as though he intended to respond, but nothing came out.

She leaned her head against Tiny to hide her smile. She'd rarely seen Maverick speechless. And she liked that she'd been the one to disarm him.

Maybe she'd have to find other ways to do so. If he taught her how to flirt, what would happen if she turned around and used his techniques on him?

Would she dare?

The very thought sent her heart into a dizzying spin. No, that would be entirely out of character for her, and he'd realize something was going on.

Yet, he'd called her *darlin'*. Surely that had to mean something. The only thing she could do was try to find out what.

6

The foal was a fine-looking colt with a dark black coat.

Maverick reclined in the hay mound that he'd shoveled into a pile so he and Hazel would have a comfortable place to sit while they observed the mama and foal.

Beside him, Hazel released a happy sigh. He'd heard it enough over the years that he didn't even need to see the satisfaction in her eyes to know what the sound meant—that she was pleased with how everything was going.

The foaling had taken long hours. Darkness had fallen and the dinner hour had passed with Clementine bringing them each a plate of the roast and potatoes she'd made. Tiny had started pacing restlessly, frequently lying down and then getting up in order to reposition the foal in the birth canal.

The water hadn't broken for several more hours after

that. But within a short time, the foal's front feet and nose had made an appearance. Then Tiny had worked hard to push the foal the rest of the way.

Hazel had needed to rupture the amniotic membrane, but otherwise Tiny had taken care of everything else. An hour later the placenta had passed. The foal had suckled at least once. Now the mother and babe were bonding.

Hazel was waiting for the foal to urinate for the first time as well as pass the meconium. But there was no hurry. Both would happen in time, especially since the newborn appeared to be healthy and strong.

Hazel hadn't needed him during the delivery. She could have handled it all by herself, even if something had gone wrong. But the plain truth was, he liked being there, liked witnessing the new life entering the world, liked seeing something so beautiful and hopeful. More than that, he liked watching Hazel work so proficiently and confidently with the mare and foal.

"You're good at the foaling," he whispered in the night air, which had grown colder with each passing hour. He'd already turned down the flame on the lantern overhead, so that now a warm glow filled the birthing area instead of the bright light they'd used earlier.

Last time he'd peeked outside, it had been snowing lightly. While snow wasn't a regular occurrence in Summit County in the spring, it happened enough that he wasn't surprised. The covering would just make it harder for the horses and the cattle to forage for feed.

Hazel stifled a yawn behind her hand. "It helps that I love what I do." She settled deeper into the hay, her hat and coat long ago discarded. Her hair hung in a single braid over her shoulder and had flipped haphazardly so that the end of it rested against his hand.

He'd been tempted to run a finger along the plait, but he'd resisted. Just as he'd resisted letting his gaze drift to her womanly figure. He'd already made that mistake once today, and he still felt the heat of desire all the way to his bones.

It was a desire he'd do well to ignore, even to pretend didn't exist. Maybe with other women, he would have allowed that desire to blaze a little. He would have flirted and let something simmer—at the most might have stolen a kiss or two.

But Hazel wasn't like any other woman. She actually wasn't like anyone else he'd ever known. And he didn't intend to let desire blaze, simmer, or anything else.

He knew from past birthings that even if he offered her a bed in the house, she'd insist on remaining with the mare and foal. She'd stay up most of the night with the newborn, keeping an eye out for any problems that might arise.

Normally, at about this point in the foaling, he'd turn in and catch a few hours of shut-eye. But tonight, for a reason he couldn't explain, he wasn't ready to head to bed. He wanted to linger in the hay beside her, watch the mama and foal, and whisper about anything.

He settled back further, kicking out his legs and crossing them at the ankles.

"You should get some sleep," she whispered.

"I'm not tired yet."

"Morning chores will come soon enough."

She was right about that. He had a whole long list of things to do that he'd been neglecting that week, including overseeing several of the stud stallions. But putting off the work one more day wouldn't hurt. "Someone's gotta keep you from sleeping on the job."

She laughed lightly and elbowed him. "I've done this more times than I can count, and I've never once fallen asleep."

"Not even to doze?"

"Well, if all is going perfectly, then sometimes I rest for a little bit."

"You're pretty amazing."

Again she laughed softly. "Thank you, Maverick. But you do know you pay me to do this, don't you?"

"Don't matter none. You did it for years without any compensation, and I reckon you'd keep doing it even if I couldn't pay you."

She shrugged, and her cheeks began to flush.

How had he never noticed that she flushed at compliments? Maybe he'd have to do it more often, just so he could watch her cheeks turn pink.

The real question that had been pestering him was how interested she really was in Ross. He'd wanted to ask her more about it, but there hadn't been an opportunity until now. "So, Ross, huh?"

"What?" Confusion edged the word.

"You got a hankering for him?"

She sat forward and buried her face in her hands. "Oh my."

"What do you know about him?" Ross was a good worker and a fine young man. But he'd only started working at the ranch last year after giving up on gold mining, and Maverick didn't know much about his past. He was gonna have to change that if Hazel was interested in him.

She shook her head, her braid swishing back and forth and bumping him.

He tugged at it. "It's a perfectly reasonable question."

"If you're my father."

"I'm practically your brother." Was he, though? The direction of his thoughts this week hadn't been brotherly.

"Brother. That's right." She dropped her hands and fell back into the mound, sending a soft cloud of dust into the air—one filled with the scent of hay. "I always really needed another brother."

In addition to Sterling, she had three other brothers. Even though two of them were currently out east attending universities, Hazel had never lacked brotherly attention. The whole Noble clan was mighty protective of their women and particular about the men Hazel and Scarlet were allowed to fraternize with.

"So, *brother*." Hazel emphasized the word a little too much. "What wisdom can you impart to your *sister*?"

"About what?" She was taking the sibling thing a little too far now. Because honestly, he didn't want to be her brother anymore, and he most certainly didn't want her to be his sister.

"We agreed you would teach me how to flirt."

Prickles of protest formed along his spine. "Ain't never agreed to that."

"It was implied."

He shook his head. "No way, no how—"

"Please, Maverick?" Her fingers brushed his arm, halting not only his words but his thoughts.

"I'm severely lacking the skills in winning a man."

"You don't need to win a man." He scrambled to form a coherent sentence with her touching him. Why was her simple touch affecting him so much all of a sudden? "The right fella needs to win you."

"It hasn't happened yet."

"It will." He wouldn't be the one to inform her that Sterling had all but threatened to castrate any of his ranch hands who even looked at Hazel or Scarlet. In fact, Sterling had made it mighty clear that none of the area miners better look at his sisters either.

Maverick hadn't complained about Sterling's carefulness when it came to Hazel and Scarlet. He felt the same way about his sisters—that there wasn't anyone who'd ever be worthy of having them as wives.

Hazel released an exasperated sigh. "I'm twenty-one, and no one has ever come courting me."

"You're plenty young."

"It's not that I'm in a hurry to get married. I love what I do here." She gave a pointed look at Tiny standing at the trough, munching on hay while her baby wobbled at her side. "But maybe it's time to start thinking about finding someone."

Why did the thought of her *finding someone* irk him?

"So teach me all you know, O wise master." Her tone was soft and teasing, as were her eyes. In fact, those bronze-colored eyes of hers were so light and warm, he felt suddenly like he was drowning in melted honey-butter.

He had to shake himself free, which was difficult since the only place he wanted to be was there, staring into her eyes the rest of the night. "I ain't gonna teach you to flirt," he whispered. "Sterling already wants to kill me. If he learns I'm filling your head with ways to seduce men, he'll not only kill me, but he'll feed me to the wild critters."

Hazel clamped a hand over his mouth and quickly

glanced around the deserted barn. The dozens of stalls were quiet on either side of the haymow, the horses at rest. Dark shadows hovered in every corner, but no one else was around to hear their conversation.

Her wide eyes turned upon him and were now filled with censure. "I'm not *seducing* anyone," she hissed.

Her hand was over his mouth. Her palm against his lips. Her fingers touching his jaw. Her skin flush with his scruff. She was right there for the taking. All he had to do was press his mouth in, and he'd get to taste her. And heaven almighty, he was suddenly hungry—no, famished—for a taste of her.

Before he could figure out how to restrain himself, he pressed into her palm with his lips and kissed the warm spot at the center.

At the contact, she froze, her gaze crashing into his and widening.

A strange and deep longing radiated through him, and he couldn't keep from kissing her palm again. She was so soft and warm and perfect, and he couldn't think of anything else that he wanted to do but keep on tasting her, especially while drowning in her eyes.

She was so beautiful, her eyes so wide, her mouth slightly open, her lips rounded with surprise.

What would it be like to kiss her lips?

Heat stabbed his gut hard, and his hands moved toward her with the need to draw her closer. He couldn't stop himself as he made contact with her hips. He skimmed the curves, settling his fingers around her waist. It would be all too easy to pull her close. Or even to lay her back in the hay and press against her.

The image sent more heat through him, and he closed his eyes to block the image, except it wouldn't go away. It was seared to the forefront of his mind.

As if those thoughts were blaring loudly for her to hear, she snatched her hand away from his mouth and scooted back several inches.

His eyes flew open in time to see not only surprise in her eyes but also confusion. She probably had no idea exactly how attractive she was and the power she could wield over a man.

"That was a flirting lesson." He spoke the first thing that came to his mind, the first excuse he could think of for why he'd just kissed her hand.

"It was?" She was holding the hand he'd kissed and grazing her thumb across the center of her palm as though trying to make sense of the kisses he'd pressed there.

"Yep. I'm gonna teach you how to flirt. But you have to promise you'll only practice with me."

"Why just with you?" Did her voice have a breathless quality to it? Had his kisses affected her as much as they had him?

"Because I'm safe and won't try to take advantage of you in return." It was the plain truth. He was safer than any other man. And the other plain truth was that he didn't want her trying out any of his tricks on anyone else. His gut tightened just *thinking* about her flirting with another man. He couldn't imagine *watching* it unfold.

She was still peering at him, her eyes wide and innocent.

"Promise you'll only flirt with me?" he persisted.

"Only with you? For how long?"

Forever? He bit back the word and instead shrugged. "Until I say so."

She cocked her head, as if she was starting to question his sanity. "Eventually I have to use what I'm learning on other men."

No, she did not. At least, not for a long time. "Some fella is gonna sweep you off your feet without you having to do a blasted thing. I guarantee it."

A small smile hovered over her lips. "Thanks, Maverick. I wish I had your confidence."

He was actually glad she was a little bit shy and reserved when it came to men. Men were intimidated by women who were shy and beautiful. And she was both.

"So, what's the first thing I should do when I approach a fellow?" She sat up straighter as though she truly were preparing to learn from the master.

"Should I call him *darlin'* the way you call all the women *darlin'*?"

"Naw, the first thing you gotta do is make eye contact." He held her gaze. "And hold it for a few seconds."

"Like this?" Scrunching her forehead, she stared at him intently, almost angrily.

He couldn't keep from grinning. "Whoa, now. We're not aiming to scare them away." Or maybe that would be a good thing.

She smiled, then swatted his arm.

"Try it again."

This time she rounded her eyes and widened her smile almost to the point of looking comical.

Another grin worked its way free. "You're not trying to make them laugh at you either."

She smacked him harder.

Before he knew it, they were both laughing, and she was making more faces and he was imitating her. He tried to teach her several more tips about smiling and winking, but she failed just as utterly with those two tasks as she had with making eye contact.

Finally, she raised her hands in surrender. "I give up. I'll never learn."

He captured her hands. "Why don't I show you. Sometimes, it's easier to learn from a demonstration."

"You are the master." Her voice was light and filled with teasing.

Before he could talk himself out of it, he twined his

fingers through hers and tugged her closer. In the same motion, he met her gaze as levelly as possible, letting himself look deeply into her eyes, holding the connection.

The playfulness in her eyes slipped away, and a strange new intensity took its place—an intensity that seemed to reach down inside and grab his heart.

Before he could say anything, her lashes fell halfway, shielding her, hiding something he didn't want to miss. But she wasn't giving him everything this time, was only sharing a tiny portion of herself, which only served to make her more alluring and even more desirable.

She was actually flirting with him perfectly at the moment, and she probably didn't even realize it, which was a good thing. Because he'd only scare her if he allowed himself to react the way he wanted to, which was to slide both hands up her cheeks, tilt her head back, and get a look more deeply into her eyes.

"How am I doing?" Her inquiry was soft, almost seductive. Or maybe he just thought it sounded that way because of what they were doing.

His attention dropped to her lips. His gut tightened with a need so powerful that he was suddenly afraid if he stayed with her in the hay, he'd do the very thing he'd told her he wouldn't do—take advantage of her.

He wouldn't do that. Absolutely couldn't.

With a burst of determination, he released her hand and pushed himself up from the hay. He paced several feet away, pinching the back of his neck and breathing hard, trying to get himself under control before he turned back around and faced the questions sure to be in her eyes.

He wasn't sure what was happening to him to stir up such desire for her. But one thing he did know—sitting there in the hay with her and flirting was like playing with fire. If he wasn't careful, he was gonna start a big blaze— one he wouldn't be able to put out. One that would hurt them both.

"You're doing too good." The word *darlin'* almost slipped out. But he wasn't gonna use it with her. She needed something special, all her own.

"Too good?" Her voice held a note of pleasure.

"Yep." He tossed her a smile and took several more steps away so that he wouldn't be tempted to fall back into the hay beside her. "You got me wanting to drop down on one knee and propose marriage to you right here and now."

She laughed lightly. "You'd never do that. But thank you for saying so."

Never? Really? He wasn't so sure about that. Something about the idea of making Hazel his didn't sound like such a bad idea. In fact, if she were his, he wouldn't have to walk away from her right now, and he could linger in the hay and pull her into his arms the way he wanted to. He could silence all her talk about learning to flirt with a long kiss—one that would teach her she was perfect just the way she was.

All the noise in his head rumbled to a stop, leaving silence in its wake along with the truth.

He liked Hazel . . . a lot.

For the past few years, every time his family had teased him about Hazel, he'd always insisted he and Hazel were just friends. But what if his family had been right? What if they'd seen his attraction to Hazel all along when he'd refused to admit it?

After tonight, how could he deny an attraction to her any longer? And did it really matter? After all, she'd never shown any interest in him. For all he knew, she'd cut and run if he ever hinted at wanting more between them.

Maybe he'd have to do a little flirting of his own with her and try to discover if she'd ever reciprocate the attraction.

Whatever the case, he had to take a break from her and cool off. Because he was learning one thing quick-like when it came to Hazel—she was hard to resist, even though she wasn't even trying to win him.

7

At a gentle caress on her cheek, Hazel stirred. Hay surrounded her and pricked her, even through her layers of clothes. A draft of cold air tickled her nose, bringing the waft of horseflesh . . . and coffee?

Where was she, and why wasn't she waking up in her bed next to Scarlet?

Another caress—this one on her forehead—drew her further into wakefulness. Her lashes fluttered up to find a broad form bent over her—long denim-clad legs, a heavy duster coat over a muscular body, and a handsome scruff-covered face.

It was Maverick. He was holding a steaming mug in one hand, and with the other he was touching her face, his finger drawing a soft line down her temple and then her cheek. His blue eyes were darker than she'd ever seen them, lingering over her face, almost as if he'd been enjoying watching her sleep.

She lifted her lashes more fully and peered up at his handsome features—squared jaw covered in a layer of dark scruff, bronzed cheeks and nose, and prominent chin that showed his strength. As if that weren't enough, his heart-stopping grin fell into place, making her stomach tumble head over heels.

He brushed his knuckles against her other cheek. "Morning, angel."

Angel?

Her pulse came to an abrupt halt. She'd never in all her days heard him call any woman by that term of endearment. Why was he doing so now?

"You're sleeping on the job." His tone held a note of teasing.

She pushed up so that she was sitting, her gaze darting to a shadowed corner of the haymow where Tiny and her foal had last been resting when she'd finally allowed herself to fall asleep. They were still there, and the foal was suckling noisily while Tiny waited, swishing her tail back and forth.

"Thought you might need this." Maverick held the mug toward her, and the scent of coffee filled her nostrils again.

"Thank you, Maverick. You're always so thoughtful." It wasn't the first time he'd brought her coffee after a long night of foaling. He truly was a sensitive man who considered the needs of others. It was just one of the many reasons why he was so irresistible.

She took the mug, wrapping her stiff fingers around it, suddenly realizing how cold the air in the barn was.

Before she could shudder, he was draping her coat over her shoulders. "Got at least a foot of snow on the ground, and it's still coming down heavy."

"Shoot." Her thoughts turned to home and the cattle that Sterling and his ranch hands had already moved to one of the north pastures. Hopefully, they'd had time to round them up and bring them back closer to the barn, where they'd be protected by the foothills, the trees, and the buildings, especially since the calves would need more shelter.

One of their first springs in Colorado, they'd learned the hard way just how dangerous a late winter snowstorm could be to the livestock. Their cattle had been grazing in an area farther out, foraging for grass left from the previous year. When the storm struck, the snow had been too heavy and blinding to round up the cattle. Many of the steers had been buried alive. Others had found places to wait out the storm and survive. But they'd lost at least forty, and it had taken several weeks before they'd tracked down the stragglers.

The serious slant of Maverick's eyes told her he was thinking about the danger too. "I'll be heading out with the fellas to drive the steers in closer."

Even though the Oakleys didn't have as many cattle

as her family, they wouldn't want to lose any of theirs either. "How far out are they?"

"Hopefully only about a quarter mile or so."

If the snow was already deep and coming down hard, it would be challenging to move the herd. But they had to bring them in closer, just in case the storm got worse. "And the horses?"

"We've spent the past couple of hours moving them in." His coat and hat were damp. Even his long, dark lashes were laden with moisture.

"So you didn't get any sleep?"

He shrugged and then cocked his head toward her hay pile. "We can't all be so lucky."

She started to climb to her feet, and he was at her side in the next instant, assisting her until she was standing. "I'll go help with the horses. We can bring some of the mares in here, and there's room in the other barn too."

He nodded. "Reckoned you'd want to do that."

She took a sip of the coffee, letting it warm her as her mind went to work finding places for as many of the horses as she could fit in the barns. By June and July, many would be sold, and they'd have plenty of room again. But this time of year, they always had a surplus and not enough stalls for all of them.

Maverick held the coffee for her while she shrugged into her coat and hat, all the while giving her more details about the conditions out in the fields. When she finished and he handed her back her coffee, she spun and began to stalk away.

"Hang on now." He snaked out a hand and stopped her. "Don't run yourself ragged."

She spun to face him again while taking another sip of coffee. "I'll be fine."

"Don't stay out there too long."

"I'm just as sturdy as any man you've got working this ranch, and you know it."

"Even so . . ."

She'd gotten the brotherly lectures from him before and knew he was just trying to keep her safe the way her own brothers would. But at times, especially after the strangely charged interactions with him lately, she was more than ready to stop being like a sister.

She tugged her arm free with more force than usual and narrowed her eyes. "I know it's hard to believe that I'm all grown up now, but I'm not your little sister anymore."

Instead of grinning and brushing off her comment with banter, Maverick moved closer so that he was boxing her in.

He was so near that she fumbled backward, bumping into the nearest stall door and nearly spilling her coffee.

With an intensity in his expression that she'd never seen before, he braced his arms on either side of her, giving her no space to sidle away from him.

She tilted her head back enough that she could watch his face and attempt to discover what he was thinking and feeling, because clearly her declaration about not being his little sister had triggered something within him.

He let his gaze drift almost languidly around her face, starting with her eyes, then moving to her cheeks, her nose, and then her chin. She had the embarrassing notion that he might drop his gaze lower, but he didn't. He shifted it to her hair, raised his hand, and gently touched a strand.

She couldn't do anything but hold her breath. What was he doing?

A second later, he pulled out a tiny piece of hay, then flicked it away.

Her heart had stopped working at some point, although she wasn't sure when. And now she could hardly think as she waited for Maverick to say something.

The blue of his eyes at so close a range was almost too powerful, too mesmerizing, making her knees weak and wobbly. If she hadn't been holding her coffee, she would have grabbed a fistful of his coat and clung to him.

He shifted his hand down and brushed his knuckles across her cheek, just as he had only moments ago when she'd been waking up. He'd never been so familiar with her before. What did it mean?

"I realize you're all grown up, angel." His tone was low, almost husky. "It's hard to miss."

He'd called her *angel* again, and her insides were melting faster than lard in an iron skillet.

"And let's get one thing real straight. I already got two sisters and don't need another one." He drew a final line down her cheek to her chin, the soft touch making her body quiver with a need she couldn't explain. He stood there a moment longer, almost as if he was debating something. Then he stepped back.

She had the very strange but real urge to launch herself against him and was grateful for the cup of coffee which kept her planted to the stall door. She guessed throwing herself on Maverick would have counted as slightly deranged and lovesick, but with every passing moment, she couldn't keep from feeling as though something had shifted between them—that their relationship was changing, that he was interested in her in a way he'd never shown before.

Or was she only imagining it all?

8

Over the course of the day, Hazel was too busy to think much more about the changes that seemed to be happening with Maverick. She had only a few moments to spare when she wasn't focused on getting the horses into stalls and out of the storm, or working with Tiny and the new foal. Even in those quiet breaks, she forced herself not to drag back out the interactions she'd had with Maverick over the past week and analyze each one.

She could admit she was afraid that dwelling on him too much would only stir up her longings all the more, just as it had done in the past. There had been many times over the years when she'd misinterpreted something he'd said or done, believing it to mean he was starting to like her only to have him ignore her for weeks after that.

After too many disappointments to count, she'd learned her lesson. Never assume Maverick meant anything beyond friendship. He was simply a friendly and nice fellow to every woman he met. And she'd never be anyone special to him, other than his best friend's sister.

By late afternoon, thankfully, the cattle were herded to safety in the pasture closest to the foothills where the tall lodgepole pines and other shrubs provided some covering for them. Maverick and the handful of ranch hands who worked for High C Ranch had separated out the cows and calves, driving them near the outbuildings for even more protection.

With at least another foot of snow having fallen throughout the day and the wind causing drifts, Hazel wasn't surprised when Alonzo didn't come after her. She hadn't expected him to be able to make it—had hoped he wouldn't try. Besides, she figured he'd be busy trying to help Sterling in any way he could. Although she was anxious to know how everyone was doing back home and whether they'd been able to save the cattle, all she could do was pray.

When darkness fell, Clarabelle was the one to finally pull her inside and convince her to stay the night in a real bed and not the barn. Hazel was too tired to resist, and let the young woman help her change into warm, dry clothing and then pamper her with a warm meal of soup and biscuits. With the snow having mostly stopped, it hadn't been long before Maverick joined them at the table, satisfied that he'd done everything he could for the livestock.

They lingered over the meal. Then afterward, Hazel went into Mrs. Oakley's bedroom to update her on the new foal and assure her that all the horses were well taken care of during the storm.

A short while later, Maverick, in fresh and dry clothing, pulled up a chair at his mother's bedside. Mrs. Oakley sat among the mounds of pillows, her robust body now frail and wasting away. Her once blond-red hair had turned gray, and her cheeks were sunken. But she beamed at them both, her thin face radiating peace.

"Your pa taught you well, Mav," she said as Maverick finished telling her about all the work they'd done to protect the livestock. "I have no doubt the ranch will prosper under your leadership, especially with Hazel's help."

In his chair beside the bed, Maverick was resting his elbows on his knees while he gently held his ma's hand in his. He gazed at her tenderly. "I don't know what I'd do without Hazel."

Mrs. Oakley nodded. "You're a good team."

Hazel, in the chair beside Maverick, smiled at Mrs. Oakley but couldn't keep from wondering if the dear woman had the wrong idea about her and Maverick being a couple. Hazel opened her mouth to clarify but then decided that if the assumption made Mrs. Oakley happy, then that's all that mattered.

"You and Pa made a good team," Maverick said.

"We sure did." Mrs. Oakley's eyes filled with a wistfulness Hazel had seen there before whenever Mr. Oakley was mentioned. Hazel had always admired the couple's marriage. Their love for each other had been so evident, especially in the way Mr. Oakley had treated his wife. His every interaction with her had been sweet and kind and considerate, as if she were more important than anything or anyone else in his life.

With that kind of love given freely and so generously day after day, what woman could resist loving that man passionately in return? Just as Mrs. Oakley had done.

She tired easily, and Hazel and Maverick didn't stay much longer before heading out into the spacious sitting area of the large cabin.

Sofas covered in colorful pillows and blankets were positioned in front of a central fireplace that was blazing and crackling with welcome heat. Glowing candles on the large log mantel added to the warmth.

Hazel had always loved the wide-open room with several bedrooms as well as the kitchen on the main floor and a loft above. She'd spent many a night giggling with Clementine and Clarabelle in the loft during sleepovers when they'd all been younger.

Now only Clarabelle joined her and Maverick in front of the hearth while Clementine took over the care of Mrs. Oakley. For a while, the three of them reminisced about the past, until finally Clarabelle yawned and stood, excusing herself with the need to go to bed.

After Clarabelle closed the door of her room behind her, Hazel expected Maverick to suggest that they go to bed too, but he didn't seem to be in a hurry. And with him sitting only a foot away on the same sofa, Hazel wasn't ready for her time with Maverick to end, even though her eyes were growing heavy.

As usual, Maverick was full of stories about everyone and everything, always animated and easy to talk to. Even though he was much too handsome sitting on the sofa nearby, she somehow managed to keep her thoughts in line, which came from years of practice.

"Do you remember that time when Sterling and me snuck up on the roof and climbed in through the loft window?" His voice held a note of contentedness, and his eyes were alight. He was sprawled out, his legs stretched out in front of himself and his arms draped over the back of the sofa.

"You snuck in on us more than one time." She loved seeing him this way, as if he didn't have a care in the world.

His grin widened. "We were good at getting in without you hearing us."

"We just pretended not to hear you because we felt sorry for you."

He lifted his hand near her head and tugged on her braid. "That's not true."

"It is true."

"What about the night we put toads in the bed? I suppose you heard us and just waited to start screaming until we were outside?" He hadn't removed his hand from her hair. Instead, he gently fidgeted with the plait.

"Maybe we didn't hear you that time. But we usually did."

He skimmed his fingers down her braid a little ways and then back up, still not letting go.

She couldn't read into his action. It didn't mean anything. Even so, her heartbeat pattered faster.

"Those were good times." His tone turned nostalgic, and he was staring into the fire, his expression growing pensive. All the while, he grazed her braid, probably not even realizing he was doing it.

She could guess why his mood was shifting . . . because he was thinking about Sterling and the friendship they'd shared. The two had always been so close with so many adventures and so many common interests.

"I'm sorry, Maverick." She leaned toward him and patted his knee. "I know the rift with Sterling is hard."

He didn't respond except to drop his other hand—the one that wasn't fingering her braid—on top of hers at his knee. He patted hers once, twice, then left it there.

She started to pull her hand away, but he grasped it more firmly, as though trying to communicate that he needed her comfort and understanding. That's all it was—her being available for him when he needed her.

"He'll eventually accept what happened," she said.

"That doesn't mean he'll ever forgive me." He brushed his thumb across her knuckles. With his hands now wreaking havoc in two places, how would she be able to concentrate enough to communicate?

Maybe if she blocked out his face, she'd be able to ignore his touch better. She closed her eyes and leaned her head back. "He's stubborn, but he's rational."

"But he's hurt real bad. And hurt can make a man sore for a long time."

"Sterling's too stubborn to let it keep him down for too long." She couldn't control the yawn that escaped.

"I oughta let you get to bed." His voice was soft, apologetic.

"I'm fine." Her eyes were growing heavy. After all, she hadn't slept much the previous night and had been on her feet all day.

"Here." Maverick shifted on the sofa toward her.

Her eyes flew open to find him drawing her in to his side and draping his arm across her shoulders. As he situated himself, he kept hold of her hand upon his knee and then let his other hand caress first her shoulder and then her upper arm before letting it dangle.

She wasn't sure what to do or how to react, so she held herself stiffly.

"Relax," he whispered near her ear. "You don't always

have to be so strong, you know."

Was that what he thought? That she was trying to be strong? She almost snorted. Little did he know how weak she truly was, especially with the way her body was reacting to being against his.

Even so, she couldn't say anything, couldn't admit just how much he affected her. So she made herself sink against him, her shoulder and arm fitting into his side so well that she felt as though she were made to be there.

What was he thinking? Was he feeling the same way?

Surely he wouldn't have initiated the contact and pulled her close if he wasn't interested in having a different kind of relationship with her. After all this time, what if she could stop fighting against her attraction to him and see what developed?

Maybe he was finally ready for more. Maybe this was just the beginning of something new between them. Maybe he wanted to get closer.

He was silent for long moments, staring ahead at the flames in the fireplace. "I oughta go over and try to talk to him."

She released an inward sigh. Maverick wasn't thinking about her and how nice she felt beside him. No, he was still distracted by his thoughts of Sterling. He probably wasn't even really noticing her presence.

She leaned her head back. She had to keep her perspective in place and remember Maverick was a womanizer through and through. If he was leading her on, it was because that's the way he was and not because he really meant anything by it.

For now, though, she closed her eyes, intending to just enjoy being with him, tucked into his side and spending time with him.

She wasn't sure how much time had passed when she awoke with a start, her eyes opening to darkness. Only a low glow remained from the fire, which had burned down to embers.

Even though her mind was hazy with sleep, her body quickly attuned to the fact that she was still on the sofa and curled into the warmth of Maverick's body.

He was leaning back with his head resting against the edge of the sofa, one leg stretched out on the cushions and one down. Somehow she'd ended up lying beside him, partially on top of him, her head resting on his chest with his arm sprawled across her.

Mortification rushed through her, and her body flushed at so indecent a predicament. She was practically sleeping with Maverick. How had this happened?

She lifted her head just slightly, enough that she could see he was resting peacefully. His eyes were closed, his expression relaxed, his breathing even. No doubt he'd been as exhausted as she'd been, and they'd simply drifted to sleep as they'd been sitting and talking.

There was nothing to worry about. She'd extricate

herself carefully and make her way up to the loft where Clarabelle had told her she could sleep.

As Hazel started to lift her hand, she halted as further embarrassment swept through her. Somehow her hand had slipped under his shirt and was now pressed against his bare abdomen.

She cringed and prayed her wandering hand hadn't made its move while Maverick had been awake, that her wayward desires had only surfaced after he'd fallen asleep.

Her fingers were splayed over his stomach. And oh my, it was some stomach. Not that she had much experience in feeling stomachs. She had none, actually. But there was no disguising the fact that Maverick had a rock-solid abdomen—one worthy of a prize for best manly stomach in the West.

A manly stomach she had no business groping.

She started to inch her hand out from underneath his shirt.

But at her slight movement, he shifted and drew her into him more securely, her head tucked under his chin. His arm tightened, almost as if he didn't want her to leave him.

She held herself motionless.

He released a sleepy breath, then he bent and pressed a kiss to the side of her head.

Her pulse halted abruptly. Was she dreaming? Or were his lips really touching her head near her temple?

The pressure ended a moment later, but he didn't move his mouth away. Instead, the warmth of his steady breathing bathed her temple, making the moment all too real.

Maverick was kissing her—or at least kissing her head. And holding her tight.

And she still had her hand up his shirt.

She closed her eyes and fought against all the strange desires that were rolling through her. She wanted him to kiss her again. Even if just on her head. She wanted to stay in his arms. She wanted to lie next to him. She wanted the freedom to touch his beautiful body.

But those were the kinds of privileges reserved for a man and wife. And Maverick couldn't even see her as a woman half the time, much less think about her as a potential wife.

She had to put an end to the closeness.

Even if she woke him up, she had to get up and go to the bed in the loft.

Taking a breath of resolve, she slipped her hand out from underneath his shirt and then started to push herself up.

She made it only halfway when both of his arms came around her, and he pulled her down on top of him, this time fully.

9

Hazel was on top of him.

Wakefulness hit Maverick, pulling him out of the half-conscious state he'd been in while resting with her on the sofa after she'd fallen asleep. To make her more comfortable, he'd reclined and situated her at his side with her head on his chest.

He'd only planned to close his eyes for a short while—hadn't intended to fall asleep. In fact, he'd debated on whether he oughta get up and carry her to the loft. But it'd been so nice having her right there by his side that, truth be told, he'd been selfish and stayed because he wasn't ready to be away from her.

Now, somehow she'd shifted positions, and every single perfect inch of her perfect body was pressing into his. He could get used to waking up to this every day.

His lips curved up into a grin. "Hey there."

Her face hovered above him, her nose brushing his.

"Maverick," she hissed his name. "You can't hold me like this. It isn't decent."

He became conscious of his arms surrounding her, his hands on her back—one awfully low but thankfully not low enough that he'd deserve a good walloping for crossing a line.

She was right. Having her on top of him wasn't decent either. As much as he liked holding her, he had no right to hug her or even rest with her on the sofa. He shouldn't have lain down with her, should have guessed he wouldn't have the willpower to resist her—not with the way his thoughts had been circling back to her every chance they had.

All last night after the foaling, his mind had been filled with her face as she'd watched the birthing with amazement, joy, and confidence. All day as he'd herded the cattle with his men, he'd thought of little else except for her, hoping she wasn't working too hard but knowing she was.

"Maverick, wake up." She wasn't making an effort to get off him, wasn't wiggling or pushing or even trying to roll away. Maybe she liked being close to him too.

"I'm awake, angel." He'd decided on calling her *angel.* It seemed to fit her, and he liked it a whole lot better than *darlin'.*

"I should get to bed." Her whisper wasn't all that demanding. Was there even reluctance in her voice?

"Before you soil my reputation."

"Since I'm soiling your reputation, I reckon we oughta just get married. What do you think?" His tone was laced with teasing, but as soon as the question was out, all humor left him. What was he saying? He wasn't really suggesting marriage, was he?

Or what if he was?

The question must have startled her too, because she grew silent and still. She lay on him only a moment longer before pushing up.

Even though he didn't want to release her, he let his arms fall away.

She climbed up until she was standing beside the sofa.

He didn't move from his spot. Instead, he crossed one arm behind his head and watched her as she fidgeted first to straighten her blouse and then her skirt—both of which she'd borrowed from Clementine or Clarabelle.

What was she thinking? How did she feel about him? About them? Maybe he didn't have any right to ask her, but he sure wanted to.

She hesitated a moment, then turned to go.

Before she could take a step away, he reached out and caught her hand. He didn't know what he was doing, didn't know what he wanted from her or even from himself. All he knew was that he couldn't let her walk away yet.

He pushed himself up and then stood, still holding her hand.

She was looking at the embers and nibbling at her bottom lip. If the room had been well lit, he guessed it would have shown flushed cheeks too. With her hair having come loose from her braid, wisps floated around her face and neck.

Heaven almighty, she was beautiful. She was so beautiful his chest began to ache just watching her. It ached with something he couldn't explain, except that he suddenly and fiercely wanted Hazel to be his.

"Hey," he whispered, unable to keep himself from reaching his other hand up and tucking one of her strands behind her ear.

She turned her eyes upon him. In the darkness he couldn't see the play of emotion there. But he could sense something, an interest in him, maybe even desire.

Without giving himself a chance to second-guess his actions, he dipped down and touched his lips to hers. He waited just a fraction, giving her permission to back away and end the kiss if it wasn't what she wanted.

But she didn't move. Instead, she waited, almost breathlessly. Was this her first kiss?

A swell of yearning rose inside him, and he pressed in more completely. As he did so, he was unprepared for the softness and warmth of her lips. And he was unprepared for her response. She lifted on her toes and met him with a sweet fervor that somehow seemed to set his blood on fire. Their meshing contained such a soft and delectable rhythm that he felt the tug of it keenly, all the way to his heart and soul.

He started to draw her closer, wanted to wrap her up in his arms, but before he could find his way out of the oblivion that her kiss had taken him to, she broke away. She backed up several steps, paused. Then she turned and raced up the stairs that led to the loft.

A moment later, the soft squeak of the bed told him that she'd lain down. Although she was quiet, he could still hear her rapid breathing and knew she'd been just as affected by their kiss.

Affected wasn't the right word for how it had impacted him. He could only stand beside the sofa, his entire world flipped upside down. His muscles were tense with need, his blood hot with possessiveness, his pulse thudding with her name.

Hazel. His woman. His and only his. For always.

He loved her. Heaven almighty he loved her, more than anyone or anything.

He almost groaned aloud with the pressure of that love inside his chest.

How had this happened so quick-like? Or what if it wasn't quick? What if it had been happening for years but he'd been too scared to admit it?

After the pact he'd made with Sterling about never liking each other's sisters, he reckoned he'd been left with little choice but to stuff away every last feeling for Hazel that might have been there to begin with.

If he was completely honest with himself, maybe he'd allowed himself to flirt like crazy with most women to distract himself from thinking about Hazel. Maybe he'd needed to keep his feelings locked away even from himself so that he wouldn't dwell on her and how much he liked her.

Whatever the case, the kiss—or something—had unleashed the feelings, and now they were flooding him with an overwhelming need to be with her. His muscles tightened with the longing to chase after her, pull her into his arms, and confess to her that he loved her.

In fact, the need to do so almost pained him.

But he couldn't go up into the loft. He didn't trust himself—not now that his bottled emotions for her were unleashed.

Instead, he lowered himself back to the sofa and perched on the edge. With his elbows on his knees, he buried his face into his hands. What was he gonna do now? There was no way he could go back to being just friends with her. But he couldn't move beyond friendship until he talked with Sterling and told him he wanted to end their no-sister pact.

But talking with Sterling at this point was about as impossible as going to the moon.

Or was it?

He sat up. Sterling thought he'd been interested in

Violet. If he went to Sterling and told him how he felt about Hazel—that he was crazy about her, loved her more than anything and wanted to marry her—what would Sterling say?

Maybe it would work to smooth things over between them. He'd be able to prove he had no feelings toward Violet and never had, that he wasn't interested in stealing her away, that the only woman he wanted was Hazel.

Maverick drew in a deep breath. Yep. Tomorrow he'd take Hazel home, and while he was at the Noble Ranch, he'd corner Sterling. He'd apologize for everything that had happened at the failed wedding and his role in it. Then he'd tell Sterling how he felt about Hazel.

After that, he'd come up with a grand way to show Hazel how he was feeling. Even if she didn't love him quite yet, he'd sensed something there. He'd do his best to woo and win her over so that, soon enough, she'd love him back.

10

Maverick slept fitfully for a few hours and was up before daybreak to check on the cattle and horses.

He worked with the ranch hands to shovel away some of the snow to open up the grass. Even then, they had to carry out the last of the stored bales of hay for both the cattle and horses.

By the time he finished, the sun was high in the sky and already melting the snow. As he headed back into the barn where they kept most of the mares and the foals, he looked eagerly for Hazel, suddenly famished for the sight of her. Even if she was busy, all he needed was a glimpse of her.

As he made his way through the very full barn where one of the ranch hands was mucking stalls, Maverick tried to make his inquiry of Hazel's whereabouts casual. He didn't want to stir up any gossip about their relationship. He wanted to do things right by her, and for now, he had to keep his feelings under a very tight lock.

He was disappointed to learn Alonzo had come in a sleigh and taken her back home. He didn't understand why Alonzo hadn't been willing to let her work another day, especially knowing she would have been well taken care of at their ranch.

Regardless, Maverick determined to go after her—ride directly to Sterling and lay out all his feelings.

But he got caught up in rescuing several steers that had wandered off and were stuck in a ravine. He and his men worked for several hours to haul the creatures up, and by the time he returned to the ranch, the evening chores were waiting for them.

With the fall of darkness and the treacherous conditions, he reckoned he'd have to wait to see her until daylight. He slept fitfully again, thinking about her all night.

When another day rolled around, he stuck close to the mare barn, waiting for her to arrive with Alonzo. But as the morning passed with no sight of her, his emotions and his body wound too tightly to concentrate on anything else. He wasn't sure how he'd lived for so many years and months without her. Now, after only one day, he was almost desperate for the sight of her.

By midday, he set off for the Noble Ranch, unable to stay away from her a minute longer. After a second day of warm sunshine, the heavy snowfall was already melting away. Although he trekked slowly and had to wade through slush and mud, the two miles were familiar and easy. He'd made the journey back and forth between their ranches hundreds if not thousands of times over the years.

As he passed through the front gate with the wrought-iron Noble Ranch sign hanging overhead, his pulse picked up speed. Even though the breeze was cold, perspiration prickled his back and his forehead. He could admit he was nervous, both at seeing Hazel again and at the prospect of talking with Sterling.

He rode down the path that led toward the barns, taking in the ranch that was much like the Oakleys', except for larger in scope. Mr. Noble had always wanted more and chased after big dreams. Sterling was just like his father with his plans for expansion and his unending need to have and do more.

Maverick didn't have that insatiable need. Although he worked hard and loved what he did, he was content with a simpler life. He didn't have a drive to become the best or greatest or wealthiest at anything.

In fact, the idea of settling down with Hazel and continuing to work the horse farm together was mighty appealing. He actually couldn't think of anything he'd like more. Ma had said they made a good team, and she was usually right about most things.

As the east pasture came into view, Maverick reined in at the sight of Sterling and his ranch hands with dozens and dozens of cattle. The cattle didn't seem worse for the wear, which meant they'd been safely rounded up from wherever they'd been grazing.

The herd consisted mostly of Herefords along with Durham bulls, but Sterling and his father had also started a new breed that was more winter hardy. So far the crossbreeds were doing well, providing a better cut of meat, and buyers were paying a premium for them.

Surrounded by the cattle, the men were pitching hay and grain from several wagons. The Nobles grew several hundred acres of alfalfa hay, had two grain silos for storage, and probably had enough to see them through until June.

Maverick homed in on his best friend—easy to do among the men since Sterling carried himself with a confidence and strength that made him a natural leader. Sterling was also taller and more muscular than the other fellows . . . and more intimidating.

Maverick hesitated, glancing toward the large Victorian-style house that graced the spread. Painted white and trimmed with black, it was elegant and refined and showcased the Nobles' success, different than the simple, homey cabin that his family had continued to live in, even though they could have built something bigger too.

He swept his gaze over the snow-covered yard, hoping for a glimpse of Hazel. Except for a maid wading through the slush and hanging linens out to dry on a clothes line, no one was in sight.

As much as he wanted to ride on to the house and see Hazel, he had to make amends with Sterling first. Hopefully, in the process, he'd be able to convince Sterling that it was time to do away with the pact they'd made long ago.

Dragging in a deep breath that was filled with the scent of damp earth and cattle, Maverick nudged his horse off the path toward the east pasture. He made it only halfway there before he was spotted. One of the ranch hands noticed him first and said something to Sterling with a nod his direction. Standing in the back of the wagon, Sterling straightened and glared in Maverick's direction, both gloved hands gripping his pitchfork as though he planned to wield it as a weapon.

Maverick slowed his approach. When he was a dozen paces from Sterling, he reined in and nodded. "Sterling."

Sterling's broad shoulders were bent, his face haggard, his demeanor hardened. "Thought I told you I didn't want to see or talk to you again."

"Reckoned we gotta work this out like grown men instead of acting like children."

The other workers had stopped pitching hay amidst the milling steers and were now watching him and Sterling with undisguised interest. No doubt everyone in Summit County and even beyond had heard of him kissing Violet on Sterling's wedding day. And no doubt everyone assumed he was guilty of betraying his best friend.

Maverick cocked his head toward the other workers. "Can we talk privately?"

Sterling didn't respond except to narrow his eyes.

Maverick bit back a sigh. His friend was a stubborn son of a gun and wouldn't make an apology easy, that's for sure. Even so, he wasn't gonna tell Sterling about his love for Hazel with all the fellows listening in. After all, he hadn't even told Hazel yet how he felt. He didn't want her hearing about it through rumors before he had the chance to make his own profession of love.

"I need just a few minutes." Maverick was unwilling to cower or beg for Sterling's time. And if Sterling couldn't respect the need for a private conversation, then he wasn't the man Maverick had come to respect.

Finally, Sterling jammed his pitchfork into the hay and hopped down from the wagon. Without a word, he stalked away from the men, dodging steers and making his way through the thick, heavy snow as if it weren't there.

Maverick slid down from his mount and followed after his friend, leading his horse and going slower.

When they were out of hearing range of the others and away from the cattle, Sterling halted and crossed his arms. "Well?"

The men on the wagons had resumed their work but were casting glances at them, clearly curious. Or maybe hoping for a fight.

The thing was, he and Sterling had never fought. Sure, there had been times when they'd irritated each other—mostly he'd been the one to irritate Sterling. But even those moments had been rare because their temperaments had balanced each other out.

Now, having Sterling peering at him with such animosity felt unnatural.

Maverick slipped off his Stetson. The moment felt too solemn, too grave, to keep it on. "About all that happened—"

"Don't apologize."

"I was just trying to get Violet back in the house—"

"I don't want to hear your excuses." Sterling spun on his heels and started to walk back to the hay wagons.

Maverick took a step after him, frustration rising inside. He had to make Sterling see the truth, had to get him to listen, even if just for a second. He scrambled to find something to say and then blurted the first thing that came to mind. "I love Hazel."

Sterling skidded to a halt in the snow.

Maverick twisted the brim of his hat. "She's the only woman I want." Hopefully his confession would help Sterling to understand that Violet never had been and never would be someone he'd be interested in.

Sterling slowly pivoted. His face was still just as stormy, if not more so.

"Violet doesn't mean anything to me."

Sterling's fists were balled.

Maverick tensed. "Her kiss meant nothin' compared to Hazel's."

"You kissed Hazel?" Sterling's tone turned brittle.

"Just once." Maverick wanted to palm his forehead. Why had he mentioned the kiss? He shouldn't have said anything about it. And maybe he shouldn't have said anything about loving Hazel either.

He could have said he liked her or had feelings for her. At the very least, he could have stuck to the matter of doing away with his and Sterling's pact. But of course, he had to make a mess of the matter.

"It wasn't a long kiss," he hurried to explain. "We fell asleep together, and it sort of just happened."

"You slept with my sister?" Sterling's voice dropped into the deadly zone.

"Not *sleep* sleep." Blast. Why hadn't he rehearsed what he would say to Sterling? Now he was only making matters go from bad to worse. "We were resting. That's all—"

Before Maverick could finish his statement, Sterling was stomping back toward him, fists raised, fury in his eyes.

Maverick braced himself for a hit. And it came a

second later. Sterling's fist slammed into his face, hitting him in the jaw. It was still sore from the last punch there on the wedding day, but Maverick didn't move. And as Sterling wound back to hit him again, Maverick squared his shoulders for another pummeling.

If it would make Sterling feel better to beat him up, then he'd let him.

Sterling held himself rigidly only a foot away. But he didn't take another swing, almost as if he'd sensed Maverick's resignation and didn't want to fight someone who wasn't willing to fight back.

The loathing that had been there on the wedding day was still there along with a heap more of it.

"C'mon, Sterling." Maverick held up his hands in surrender. "I'm mighty sorry for everything that happened last week."

"You're not sorry."

"I am. And I'll do anything to prove it to you."

Sterling lowered his fist, but his whole body remained taut and ready for a brawl. "Anything?"

Maverick hesitated and then tried for a smile. "Well, I ain't gonna rob a bank for you, if that's what you were thinking."

Sterling didn't smile in return.

Maverick's humor faded. "You know I'd take a bullet and die for you if necessary." When they were younger, they'd talked about dying for each other if they ever had to fight in a war together. Though they were older now, Maverick still felt the same way.

Sterling's Stetson cast a dark shadow over his face. "If you want to prove you're sorry, then leave me and my family alone."

Leave him and his family alone? Even Hazel? "That's ridiculous—"

"I knew you wouldn't do it." Sterling spat the words. "Because you're too selfish. Everything has to be about you."

"No it doesn't."

"Then show me." Sterling held his gaze, daring him. "Stay away from Hazel. Far away."

Maverick's insides churned. This was his chance to redeem himself in Sterling's eyes. But what his friend was demanding was too difficult. "There has to be some other way—"

Sterling scoffed. "Don't tell me you'd take a bullet and die for me—"

"I'll do it." He owed it to Sterling to do anything his friend asked of him. Not pursuing Hazel would hurt as much as taking a bullet. And it would definitely be dying to himself and his desires.

Maybe Sterling wasn't being fair to require that kind of sacrifice. But the fact was, Maverick knew he'd had a part in ruining his friend's wedding day and undermining the relationship with Violet. And since he'd caused

Sterling the misery of a broken heart, then he oughta be willing to suffer a broken heart now too.

Without waiting for Sterling to say anything else, Maverick mounted and started back the way he'd come. With every jolting step of his horse, the pain of walking away from Hazel jarred him more until his heart felt as though it had been ripped from his chest and thrown into the middle of a cattle stampede.

11

Maverick had been avoiding her. There was no other explanation.

Hazel rubbed down Candy in the paddock, but her attention was focused on the north pasture, where Maverick had been all day. Now, at the sight of him upon his gelding riding with another fellow, her heart gave a traitorous beat.

It was one week since he'd kissed her that night she'd stayed at High C Ranch and had fallen asleep with him on the sofa. Ever since then, he'd barely spoken more than a dozen words to her.

The morning after the kiss, she hadn't wanted to return home when Alonzo had come for her. But when he'd said that her family was worried about her, she'd reluctantly gone. Besides, she owed it to her family to help them too.

When she'd returned to the Oakleys' the following

day at midday, Maverick had already been gone, scouting for fresh pasture for the herds, anything that wasn't covered in snow. Once he'd located a place on the open range, he'd taken turns with the other ranch hands guarding the cattle from predators and thieves.

Then he'd been traveling for two days. She'd had to ask Clarabelle where he'd gone, learning that he'd ridden up past Dillon to check on purchasing another stud.

He'd returned late yesterday. While he'd been riding up the lane, mud-splattered but never more handsome, her heart hadn't stopped pattering with need—the need to just have one smile directed her way, one glance, even one tiny word.

But he'd ridden past the mare paddock as if he hadn't noticed she existed, and she'd gone home with Alonzo yesterday feeling as though her heart were breaking. Only when she'd finally been alone later in her room had she allowed herself to cry.

After she'd finished, she'd given herself a stern rebuke about the reality of her situation. The truth was that their kiss hadn't meant as much to Maverick as it had to her. She was obviously making far more out of the moment than he'd intended.

She should have known better with how flirtatious Maverick was with women. In fact, he probably didn't even remember the tender moment—probably had already put the kiss from his mind.

Because obviously, he'd kissed plenty of women in his life, and what was one more woman and one more kiss? Especially from someone as inexperienced and naïve as she was, who'd never been kissed and most likely had botched the entire thing.

If anything, she ought to be glad he'd forgotten about her and put the incident from his mind. It was probably better that way—less embarrassing for them both.

Candy gave a nervous whinny and sidestepped away from Hazel.

She placed a steadying hand on the mare's spotted withers. A pale gold, the horse looked as though someone had splattered ink over her hindquarters. "You're okay, girl. Everything will be just fine."

It was the mare's first foaling. At two—now almost three—she was young to be having a foal. But she was one of the first of the new Oakleys born on the ranch, so her baby was important in the continued development of the breed.

Hazel's attention drifted again toward Maverick drawing closer. Now she recognized the young man riding beside him as Tanner, one of the Oakleys' adopted sons. She hadn't seen Tanner around much, not since Mr. Oakley's death. Even before that, Tanner had been the wanderer of the family, gone much of the time up in the mountains hunting and trapping and sometimes working as a trail guide.

Tanner had a recent falling out with his older brother, Ryder. Hazel didn't know all the details of what had transpired between the two but heard it had something to do with their past.

Even if their feud didn't make sense to her, she suspected that maybe Tanner was also embarrassed that Ryder had gotten one of Captain Moore's daughters pregnant. Just as soon as Ryder had learned Sadie was carrying his baby, he'd done the honorable thing, and they'd gotten married in February.

After the quick wedding, the Oakley family had rallied around him when he'd claimed a homestead near Frisco, helping him to build a cabin and barn for him and his new wife. She was due in the early part of the summer, and everyone was hoping the birth of the grandchild would help cheer Mrs. Oakley.

Hazel glanced across the paddock to where Tiny and her foal stood together in the warm afternoon sunshine. At a week old, the colt was nursing well, already gaining weight, and starting to frolic with some of the other colts.

Now it was Candy's turn to foal. And the inexperienced broodmare would need a little more coaxing and help than Tiny.

Hazel rubbed the mare's abdomen, checking and rechecking all the signs that she might be in labor. "I don't think it'll be tonight, sweet love." Hazel brushed a kiss against the mare's cheek.

As Maverick and Tanner slowed their mounts in the yard, she stood back from the mare. Maverick was wearing his usual black Stetson, flannel shirt, and denims. But Tanner had on a coonskin cap over his brown hair and was wearing a Native buckskin coat with fringes on each shoulder.

At the sight of her, Tanner whistled and waved. "There she is. The most gorgeous woman in the Rockies."

Hazel smiled in response. Tanner was like Maverick in his ability to flirt, maybe even better. He didn't mean anything by it, the same way Maverick didn't ever mean anything. They were both just friendly young men who liked women but who clearly didn't like commitment.

She could feel Maverick's gaze upon her, and even though she wanted to exchange a familiar smile with him, the hurt was too fresh to ignore. Even if he hadn't meant to hurt her, even if he'd just been himself, she'd allowed herself to believe his attention had meant more. Now she needed a little more time to force all her feelings for him back down inside so that she could see him as nothing more than a friend again.

If only she hadn't let him kiss her. Her thoughts returned to the night of the kiss, the way he'd dipped down and pressed his lips to hers. At first she hadn't known what he was doing. The brush of his lips had been so tender, so sweet, so unexpected. He'd paused for a moment, as though giving her a chance to back away, to put an end to the kiss.

Of course she hadn't wanted to. She'd always secretly dreamed of kissing Maverick, although in her dreams she'd been the one to jump into his arms and initiate the kiss. She'd never dreamed he'd kiss her first. Why would he?

And why had he? Was it because they'd been lying together on the sofa? Had he felt close to her in the moment?

She could admit that she'd broken the kiss and run away from him because she'd been frightened. She'd been afraid of this very thing happening—where he kissed her casually, where it didn't mean anything to him, where he went on with his life unaffected. Unlike her, for whom his kiss had been earth-shattering, had kept her awake for hours that night, and had filled her thoughts for days afterward.

It still consumed her, but she was doing better today than she had been the rest of the week. She was finally making peace with the fact that she had to put him out of her mind once and for all. If she took nothing else away from the kiss, she was learning her lesson that Maverick would never see her the way she saw him.

It was for the best if she didn't allow herself to get close to him again. No more spending time with him, especially alone. No more long conversations. No more allowing him to help with the foaling—unless there was a problem. No more letting herself admire him. And certainly no more kissing. Never, ever again.

She would focus on Tanner. Maybe she could even practice some of the flirting techniques that Maverick had taught her. Not that she was interested in Tanner. She wasn't any more interested in him than she was in Ross. But if Maverick could flirt so shamelessly, then she could too.

"Hi, Tanner." She offered the young man a smile, looking him straight in his eyes the way Maverick had instructed her. "It's been a while. How are you?"

Tanner's grin widened. "At the sight of you, I'm mighty fine now."

"I've sure missed you." She hoped her smile was warm and inviting. "Things are never the same without you around."

"Well, now. You're as sweet as you are pretty. Isn't that right, Mav?"

"Yep." His answer was curt, almost as if he was upset with her.

If anyone should be upset, it ought to be her. After all, he'd been the one to kiss her and then ignore her all week.

She made herself laugh lightly, her mind scrambling to find something—anything—that would get Maverick's attention. She didn't stop to analyze why she wanted his attention, why it was so important in the moment.

Instead, she swiped off her hat and let her hair tumble down. While she'd taken the time that morning to tie it up into a messy knot, over the course of the day, it had come loose, so that now it swirled in wavy masses every which way.

She gave the thick mane a shake, feeling the stares of both men. What was Maverick thinking? Did he find her pretty with her hair down? Was the tactic working to make him take notice of her?

Even though she wanted to take a peek at him, she widened her smile and kept her attention on Tanner. "I've got an Oakley ready to foal soon. If you want to help me, she'll probably go into labor tomorrow night."

Tanner nodded. "She's the yearling?"

"Candy. The Oakley that Clementine named after she ate up a batch of the candy left outside to cool."

Tanner surveyed the mare, then glanced at Maverick as though gauging his reaction to her request.

Maverick's expression was guarded, without the usual flirtation or humor. His jaw flexed tensely, and his eyes were narrowed upon Tanner.

Tanner held up his hands as though he was afraid of being shot. "Hey now. She invited me. I can't say no to such a grand opportunity, can I?"

"Thought you were gonna help me sort through the studs." Maverick's answer was solemn and filled with accusation.

"If we do that tomorrow, we'll be done in time for the foaling."

Hazel had been attending to foalings long enough to learn that most mares waited until the quiet and privacy of night to start foaling. She didn't know how they could plan it that way, but daytime foalings were an exception and not the rule. And Maverick knew it, which meant there was no way he could object to Tanner helping her.

As though recognizing the same, Maverick pursed his lips together, and then without another word, he nudged his horse toward the barn entrance.

Tanner watched Maverick's retreating form with a growing smile. "It sure is fun riling him up."

Hazel wrapped up a fistful of hair and then began winding it back toward the top of her head. She didn't see the humor or fun in the interaction the same way Tanner did. Now, after seeing Maverick and having him ignore her again, she felt even worse.

He'd seemed almost angry with her. Maybe this past week, he hadn't just gone about his business as usual as she'd thought. Maybe he was upset about the kiss. Maybe he blamed her for it—which would be preposterous, because he'd been the one to initiate it.

But why else was he going out of his way to be cold and unfriendly toward her?

She finished her afternoon chores with the mares and foals, and as she studied her chart of the rest of the mares and their foalings hanging next to the barn door, she half listened for Alonzo and the wagon. From what she could tell, she'd have two mares ready to give birth next week, two the week after that. But during May, the foalings would grow more infrequent.

At the crunch of footsteps in the hay behind her, she tossed a glance over her shoulder to find Maverick approaching from the rear barn door. Even though he was wearing his Stetson, the furrows in his brow were deep and easy to see in the shadows.

He was still angry about something.

At the sight of her, he veered his steps toward her, as if he'd come into the barn intending to speak with her directly. If so, that would be the first time all week.

She fidgeted first with her hat, then her coat. Now that he was ready to talk, she wasn't sure she was ready to hear what he had to say.

His stride was hard and purposeful.

Her stomach cinched. She didn't want to hear him say that he hadn't liked their kiss, that he wished it hadn't happened, that he was sorry about it. She moved into the door and peered down the wooded lane. Alonzo wasn't in sight.

She started to step outside anyway, needing to get away from Maverick.

"Hazel, wait," he called.

Her stomach flipped with the urge to keep him from

saying whatever he was on a mission to say, but she only made it two steps away from the barn before his hand closed about her arm and drew her to a halt.

She didn't fight against his hold, although she knew she should. Instead, her skin warmed under his touch, his strength sending a current through her, making her insides quiver with the longing to have both his hands upon her and not just one.

She closed her eyes against the desire. "Hello, Maverick. What can I do for you?" She tried to keep her voice calm.

"I want you to stop flirting with Tanner." His demand came out low, almost a growl.

Frustration fueled into a hot flame inside her. Pulling her arm out of his grip, she spun around so that she was facing him. "You have no right to tell me who I can flirt with."

"I taught you, so I get some say."

His answer was so silly and illogical, she almost laughed. "Maybe I like Tanner and want to gain his attention."

Maverick's eyes were stormy. "Do you like him?"

"What does it matter to you if I do?" A part of her willed him to say that he cared about her and didn't want her to like any other man. But she knew he didn't, that she'd simply allowed her girlish feelings to surface and influence everything.

He released a tight sigh. "Tanner's my brother, and I love him. But he's not the right man for you."

"And I suppose you're the expert in knowing what kind of man I need?" She silently dared him to say yes, that he was well aware of the kind of man she needed. Him.

But he shook his head. "I know it's not Tanner."

"Tanner is sweet, funny, and likes me."

"He doesn't love you."

"Maybe I don't need love."

This time he grasped her arm and tugged her back into the barn. There was an urgency in his movement that made her pulse accelerate and her insides flutter. As always, she couldn't resist him, even though a part of her warned that she should.

Once they were standing in the shadows and out of the view of the barn door, he took a step toward her, closing the distance so that he was mere inches away.

His presence was as magnetic as always, and before she did something really stupid, like throw herself against him, she took a step back, pressing into the barn wall.

Again, he stepped after her so that only inches separated them. He reached out and braced a hand against the wall beside her head, and his gaze made a circuit around her face before landing on her mouth.

What was he doing? Was he thinking about kissing her again?

Delicious heat pooled low in her stomach. She'd chastised herself severely all day about her feelings for Maverick and the need to stop caring about him, but now that he was here and so close, every thought flew from her mind except one—how much she wanted him. She wanted to feel his mouth taking command of hers, wanted the pressure of his body leaning into her, wanted the tangle of their limbs and lips.

His breathing seemed to grow shallower in the space between them.

Did her nearness stir up longings in him too?

He tilted in just a little closer, his broad chest brushing hers.

The graze only sent more heat spilling through her.

Something was there between them, whether either of them acknowledged it or not. She wanted to say something about it, but the words were lost in a haze of strange desire.

As he bent his head closer, her body tightened with need—the need for another one of his kisses. She suddenly needed it more than another breath of air. Her lungs seized, as though agreeing with her. And she waited breathlessly.

But instead of moving toward her lips, he shifted so that only his cheek brushed hers, his stubble scratching her.

The sensation of his face against hers was so exquisite

she could only close her eyes and savor the closeness. And of course, she couldn't keep from wishing that the moment would never end, that she could stand in Maverick's presence like this forever.

He drew in a ragged breath, one close to her ear. "You do need love, Hazel," he whispered. "You deserve it more than anyone I know."

"What about you?" Her whisper came out more of a plea, but she couldn't help herself. She wanted to know if he'd ever consider loving her.

At her whispered words, he froze. Then he pushed away from the wall and away from her. Anguish creased his face—an anguish that he quickly worked to hide.

She didn't realize she was trembling until she pressed farther back and her fingers made a connection with the barn wall. What was going on? Why was he acting this way—seeming to want her one moment and then letting her go in the next?

At the rumble of a wagon nearing the barn, she knew Alonzo had arrived and that she needed to go out before he caught sight of her alone with Maverick. Even though Sterling hadn't stopped her from coming to work at the Oakleys', he'd made sure she was well aware of his loathing of Maverick. Just yesterday, he'd even quizzed her about her interactions with Maverick, asking her how much time she was spending with him.

She'd been able to honestly answer that she'd hardly

seen him all week and that he hadn't talked with her or spent any time with her.

If Alonzo carried home word that she'd been in the barn alone with Maverick and that they'd been standing awfully close, close enough to kiss, Sterling would accuse her of lying and do everything within his power to force her to quit her job.

Because even after almost two weeks since the failed wedding, he was still bitter and angry and showed no signs of being able to forgive Maverick.

And the truth was, she was more confused than ever about what was happening between herself and Maverick. After the past week of hardly any interaction and feeling shoved aside, what did this closeness now with him mean?

She finally let herself meet Maverick's gaze. For just a second, his eyes seemed open, like windows, letting her glimpse deep inside. Heat and attraction and even something more glowed there.

But with a quick shake of his head, he shuttered himself off. "Stay away from Tanner." Then he spun and stalked off.

As she watched him, she wanted to shout that *he* needed to stay away from *her*, that every time he came near, it hurt even more when he walked away. Surely it would be easier on her heart if she cut him out of her life and stopped caring about him altogether.

If only she could.

12

"When will you admit you love Hazel?" Tanner's question echoed in the quiet kitchen.

In the middle of taking a sip of his coffee, Maverick choked, then spluttered coffee across the table.

Tanner's grin only kicked up, as if he'd gotten the reaction he'd been shooting for.

Maverick ducked his head so that Tanner couldn't read the truth in his expression and eyes. He was thankful Clarabelle was feeding Ma her breakfast and Clementine was out doing laundry.

He was also relieved at times like this that his pa had always provided their ranch hands with separate living quarters and their own cook, so that their family could have privacy and remain close . . . or at least, they had remained close while Pa was alive.

Just this past Christmas, they'd all been home and had filled the large kitchen table. Even Weston, his oldest brother, and his new wife Serena and their little boy Tate had ridden up from Fairplay to be there. During the celebration, they'd laughed and joked and talked with all the boisterousness and love that had always been present in their family.

That was the last time they'd all been together.

Maverick sighed, feeling the weight of his pa's death all over again. Even his ma's absence in the kitchen was hard to get used to. Although the room was still cheerful with its white furniture, wide window, and colorful curtains and wall hangings, it never felt quite right without Ma there.

"So?" Tanner held his mug to his lips, his eyes filled with knowing.

Maverick set his coffee down with more force than necessary. "My relationship with Hazel is none of your business."

Tanner rolled his eyes as he took a big slurp.

Maverick reached for another sweet roll from the plate Clementine had left at the center of the table. The yeasty aroma of the rolls along with sugar and cinnamon lingered in the morning air with the scent of the coffee.

He wasn't hungry for more, especially after the eggs, sausage, and toast Clementine had already fixed. But he knew his sister was trying to make things seem as normal as possible, especially now with the strained relationship with the Nobles.

He hadn't told anyone about his conversation with Sterling earlier in the week—hadn't wanted to upset his family any more than they already were about everything. A part of him wanted to mention something to Hazel about riding over to talk to Sterling and trying to get permission to pursue her. But he hadn't wanted to put her in a position where she had to choose between him and Sterling. That wouldn't be right either.

Instead, he'd steered clear of her. From what he could tell yesterday when he'd ridden up with Tanner, she was hurt and probably confused by his brusqueness. No doubt she'd wondered what their kiss had meant.

Maverick exhaled heavily.

Now it appeared she was ignoring him in return.

She'd also obviously learned her first flirting lesson well, from the way she'd unleashed her womanly charm on Tanner. The eye contact, the smiles, even taking off her hat and letting her hair down had all been excellent tactics. The whole time, Maverick had stewed inside, hating that she was using her wiles on Tanner and not on him.

She'd been so stunning with all her fair hair cascading over her shoulders in the sunlight that he'd been irrationally jealous yesterday that Tanner had gotten to see her with her hair down like that.

Tanner took a final swig from his coffee, then pushed back from the table and stood. "Guess if you don't love her, then you won't mind if I have a little fun with her."

"Whoa, now." Maverick shot up from his chair. "Don't you dare go near her." That same irrational jealousy came roaring back like a beast let loose from its cage.

Tanner shrugged. "If you're not claiming her, then she's fair game for anyone."

"She's off-limits, especially for you." Maverick fisted his hands, ready to take a swing if necessary to prove his point.

"No. Sorry." Tanner reached for his coonskin cap on the peg near the back door. "You don't have a right to prevent her from finding happiness with someone else."

Maverick's muscles tightened, but he kept his fists at his side. Tanner was right. Except that Maverick didn't want her to find happiness with anyone else besides him.

But with Sterling's ultimatum, what could he do? He had to prove to his friend that he valued their relationship, that he wasn't selfish, that he hadn't meant to interrupt the wedding with his foolishness. If staying away from Hazel would repair his friendship, then he had to do it, didn't he?

Tanner shoved his arms into his coat. "You've had it bad for Hazel for years. Don't know why you can't see it."

"I see it."

Tanner froze and turned to face him, his grin fading.

With the admission hanging in the air between them,

Maverick swallowed hard, pushing down a sudden swell of trepidation. There was no more hiding his feelings about Hazel from anyone, least of all himself.

Tanner's lean features were browned and roughened from all his time out in the wilderness. Even so, he had a tenderness that softened the lines from time to time, and now was one of those times. "If you see it, then it's time you do something about it."

"It's complicated."

"How complicated is it to tell a woman you love her?"

"Sterling told me to stay away from her."

Tanner didn't respond for a moment, his expression uncharacteristically solemn, giving him a gentlemanly quality. At such times, Maverick imagined that Tanner's and Ryder's real parents had been fine folks. Course, nobody knew because the two had been abandoned as little boys and raised in an orphanage for many years.

"I know you count Sterling as your closest friend," Tanner said, clearly choosing his words carefully, having heard from Clementine and Clarabelle a repeat of the wedding day during supper last night. "But a real friend wouldn't make you pick between him and the woman you love."

Under other circumstances Maverick would have agreed with Tanner. But after the ruined wedding and his role in it, he couldn't shed the guilt or the feeling that he owed it to Sterling to make up for the heartache he'd caused.

At a sudden loud and frantic banging on the front door, Maverick's long steps took him quickly through the kitchen and into the front room. He made it to the door before Clarabelle could reach it.

Gone was the carefree expression of youth. Now her pretty face was wreathed with worry. With the loss of Pa and now Ma's sickness, his sisters were having to grow up too soon. And all he'd ended up doing was making matters worse.

As he swung open the door, he took a step back at the sight of Hazel standing on the raised front porch in her usual Stetson, coat, and corduroy skirt, her eyes wide and troubled.

His heart began to thud hard. Something had happened to her. "You all right?"

"I'm fine. It's Candy. I can't find her anywhere since I arrived."

Maverick's heart slowed its pace, and relief eased through him. Nothing was wrong with Hazel. And that was really all that mattered.

"She probably got nervous about the foaling." Hazel's forehead was furrowed as she scanned the property to the west.

"Bet she found a hidden nook somewhere around the ranch."

"I searched every place I could think of, and I didn't see her."

Maverick gave Hazel what he hoped was a reassuring nod. "I'll be right out, and we'll find her."

With Tanner's help, they searched each barn and outbuilding. But with no sign of the mare anywhere, they spread out and widened the scope of their hunt. Maverick and Hazel skirted the pines that bordered the house while Tanner headed the opposite direction.

They scoured the woodland but saw no hint of her. As they headed back into the ranch yard, Tanner's whistle and wave from the far end of the west pasture beckoned them. Hazel started jogging toward him, and Maverick followed.

As they reached Tanner, Maverick could see the gap in the barbed wire and guessed Candy had escaped through the opening.

"The barbed wire was cut." Tanner was kneeling just outside the west gate and was brushing aside grass, probably looking for tracks.

Maverick halted beside Hazel and bent to study the opening in the wire. The area was narrow, but it was wide enough for a slender horse to slip through. The slices in the wire were sharp and clean, too, which meant the fencing hadn't broken on accident. Tanner was right— someone had cut it.

Maybe the horse thieves were back.

Maverick straightened, his hand landing on his revolver. He surveyed the cottonwoods that grew alongside the Blue River and then the shrubs and scraggly junipers that dotted the lowest hills. Large clumps of snow remained in the shadowy places, but otherwise the terrain was mostly dry. And no one was in sight.

But that didn't mean the horse thieves weren't there hiding.

The nightmare from January came rushing back, a frigid morning when they'd awoken to find that a dozen of their horses were gone. The barbed wire had been cut then too. Since the ground had been covered in snow, the tracks of the horse thieves had been easy to spot, and it had been clear they'd taken the horses to the north, likely with the intention of getting them to the easier passes that would allow them to drive the horses to the markets in Denver.

Pa hadn't wanted to chase after thieves, had suggested they report the incident to Sheriff Shade in Breckenridge and let him form a posse to go after the stolen livestock.

But Maverick had thought he was invincible, and he'd been filled with too much pride about his own abilities to track and fight. When he'd insisted on going out a short way to at least identify the thieves, Pa had insisted on riding along.

Maverick had reasoned that the thieves wouldn't be able to go fast or far with the terrain covered in snow. He'd been right and had easily tracked them to a gulch near Frisco. Once he and Pa had assessed their opponents,

Pa had wanted to head back.

But with the stolen horses in full view and out in the open, Maverick had wanted to wait another hour until darkness fell, hoping to grab several of their best and take them back home. Course, he hadn't thought through the ramifications.

He closed his eyes to block out the memories, but they came anyway. The moment he'd inched out of hiding and made his way toward the horses, the thieves had started shooting at them. Unfortunately, he and Pa had been outnumbered and pinned down with no easy way out of the gulch. As the hours had dragged by and the temperatures began to drop, their situation had grown dire.

Finally, Pa had decided he'd cause a distraction so that Maverick could make it down the ravine and go after help. Maverick hadn't wanted to leave Pa behind, but since he'd been a sharpshooter in the war, Pa would be able to defend himself easily enough.

And maybe Pa would have . . . if the shower of bullets from the thieves hadn't started an avalanche in the cliffs right above him.

Maverick opened his eyes and shook his head, trying to clear his thoughts of the image of the sheets of snow and ice tumbling down the hillside directly toward his pa. Even though it had been dark, the moonlight had been bright enough to illuminate the danger. He'd shouted at his pa to run, but Pa'd had only seconds, enough time to glance at the avalanche headed his way, then nod goodbye to Maverick.

He'd been buried under a mountain of snow and ice. Even though Maverick had tried to dig him out, the darkness, the weight of the snow and rocks, and the gunfire from the thieves had made the task nearly impossible. He'd ridden back to the ranch, rounded up as many men as possible, and gone back out to the gulch.

By then, the horse thieves had escaped. But retrieving the stolen horses hadn't mattered anymore. All that'd mattered was uncovering Pa and praying for a miracle that he'd somehow survived.

At dawn, they'd finally found his body, pale and lifeless. From what they could tell, he'd been knocked unconscious—hadn't suffered much, possibly even died instantly.

Everyone else had blamed the horse thieves, but Maverick held himself responsible. If only he hadn't been so proud or impulsive. If only he hadn't insisted on having his way. If only he'd listened to Pa and turned back and waited until they had more help.

But no, he'd pushed forward with what he'd wanted to do. Had been just as selfish then as he'd always been, seeking the thrill and the glory without considering anyone else.

Tanner was examining the ground carefully, already

several dozen paces away from the broken fence, with Hazel following close behind. He halted and peered to the foothills to the northwest of the ranch. "From what I can tell from the hoofprints, your mare headed up into Dead Man's Gulch."

With his spine prickling, Maverick again scanned the foothills for signs of any horse thieves lingering about. "How many did the horse thieves get this time?"

Tanner bent and pushed back more of the dead damp grass. "Only one set of prints out here today."

"So Candy is alone?" Hazel asked.

"Looks that way."

Maverick poked at the dangling wire. "Then who cut the fence?"

Tanner shrugged. "Maybe it's been cut for a while, and you just didn't notice it."

"Or maybe the horse thieves are back in the area looking to steal more horses." Course, with everything that had happened, they'd all but given up finding their stolen horses. After the funeral and once Pa had been buried, the sheriff had done the best he could to follow all leads. But the thieves and the horses had never been seen again.

With narrowed eyes, Tanner followed the horse prints for a dozen more paces.

"Any idea what happened?" Hazel anxiously scanned the area ahead for the mare. Boulders and shrubs and clumps of dead grass covered the barren slope.

"The hoofprints belong to a mare carrying the extra weight. I have no doubt she's your mare, and I also have no doubt she was looking for a private place to do her foaling. She's probably not too far up the gulch."

Hazel nodded, then started hiking in the direction of Dead Man's Gulch.

"Whoa, now." Maverick trotted after her, easily catching hold of her arm and bringing her to a halt. "You can't just hike up there."

Hazel's expression was set with the determination he loved. Except that right now, he had no intention of letting her run off into the gulch looking for the mare. Not by herself, horse thieves or not.

Hazel's eyes radiated distress. "Candy might be in trouble."

"And we'll go after her, but first we gotta get our mounts and supplies."

"I'll be going by foot."

"We'll need to ride. Ain't no telling how far up the gulch she went."

Hazel crossed her arms and lifted her chin a notch. "I'm sure she's not far."

"Reckon we can go faster—"

"No, Maverick. I'm not riding."

"You can ride with me."

"No." Her tone held a finality that stopped his next sentence.

He'd known Hazel didn't ride. In all the years they'd been friends, she'd always refused—only ever went places by wagon or foot. Sterling had once told him that Hazel's fear of riding stemmed from the time she'd gotten lost while traveling west across the prairies with her family. Course, Sterling hadn't expounded much. And Maverick hadn't really thought about it much over the years—had accepted that Hazel loved the horses but never rode them.

But today, at this moment, he'd expected her to see the urgency of the situation and make an exception.

Tanner was watching their interaction. "I'd offer to go with you, but I have to head out."

"We'll be fine," Maverick said.

"You'll have no trouble. The mare won't have gone far in her condition."

"See?" Hazel broke away from Maverick's grip. "If we weren't wasting time arguing, we'd probably be halfway there."

Maverick had half a notion to go get his horse and toss Hazel over the saddle whether she wanted to ride or not. But the plain truth was, her comfort and wellbeing were more important than Candy and the foal. If Hazel didn't want to ride, he wouldn't force her.

"Reckon at the very least, I oughta bring my mount along to haul the supplies we need."

Hazel opened her mouth as though to disagree, but then she closed it and nodded. She knew as well as he did that they needed a few basic medicinal supplies and instruments just in case anything went wrong during the foaling.

Course, he was bringing along his rifle and his pa's. He wasn't planning to be caught unaware or get trapped again.

He'd made one too many mistakes already in his life and didn't want to make any more, especially any that might endanger Hazel.

13

She was a silly ninny. That's what.

Hazel followed after Maverick and his gelding, letting him lead the way deeper into Dead Man's Gulch as he followed hoofprints, droppings, and other signs of Candy's trail.

But after traveling for a good hour by foot and still not finding the mare, the anxiety inside Hazel was pulsing with greater intensity. And she'd started berating herself for not being willing to ride a horse so that they could travel faster and cover more ground.

But just the thought of sitting atop the horse stirred bile inside her and sent a bitter taste to the back of her throat. Even with Maverick near, she couldn't imagine herself riding.

The truth was, she'd made peace long ago with the fact that she would never mount a horse again. And most of the time, she didn't think about the disadvantages of not riding.

But today . . . at this moment, she was afraid her reticence would hurt Candy.

She could only hope the mare hadn't foaled yet and had simply gone off to prepare for the birth. After all, yesterday during the examinations, Candy hadn't been completely ready. Yet, if the mare had already foaled and had faced any sort of trouble, Hazel didn't want to be too late to help.

"How much longer do you think we have?" Hazel couldn't stop the inquiry. No doubt Maverick was annoyed not only by her resistance to riding but also by such a stupid question.

Instead of scoffing at her question, Maverick paused and peered around. "My guess is that she took shelter in the thicket ahead."

Dead Man's Gulch had been a playground during their growing-up years, and Maverick was familiar with each twist and turn. Even though it was in the foothills to the west of the High C Ranch, it veered north and followed along the Blue River leading to the Noble Ranch. If they went much farther, they might even end up on Noble land.

The rocky terrain was covered in moss, and a few spruce and fir trees had pushed through the granite and grew in clusters. They'd already passed a group of mountain sheep—bighorns—climbing nimbly among the higher rocks. Several rams had the heavy horns that curled around their faces, but most were ewes with their young lambs.

Maverick's hand had hardly let go of his revolver during the entire hike. His back had remained rigid, and he'd been preoccupied with scanning the landscape.

She guessed he was nervous about venturing off the ranch after all that had transpired with the horse thieves and his pa's death, but he wasn't letting his anxiety stop him. If he was able to face his fear with such bravery, wasn't it time for her to do the same?

"I'm sorry for refusing to ride." She offered the apology softly, wishing even now that she could make herself climb astride his mount but not knowing if she really could.

"I understand." He replied just as quietly, still scanning the area.

"I'm not proud that I'm so scared to get on a horse."

He shot her a quick look over his shoulders, his eyes warm with compassion. "Reckon we all got our issues."

She didn't need to have him spell out his. She could see them well enough every day. The guilt he felt over his pa's death, the guilt he carried for his ma's deterioration, and even the guilt for the trouble with his siblings. She'd wanted to soothe away the lines in his forehead more times than she could count and tell him he wasn't to blame for anything that had happened, but she suspected he'd only toss aside her platitudes.

No, the best way to help him was simply by walking by his side and helping bear his burden as best she could.

She was relieved that so far during their hike, everything between them had seemed normal again, as if nothing had happened—no kiss, no attraction, and no hurt feelings.

If only they could go back to simple friendship.

"Sterling once told me you got lost during the journey here to Colorado." Maverick's voice held an invitation to talk about the incident.

She didn't like to dredge up the memories. She'd had nightmares for years and had found that it was easier to leave the past behind her. Yet if Maverick wanted to hear about the story from her, shouldn't she be willing to share at least a little? If the roles had been reversed, she would have wanted the same openness.

"You don't have to say anything." He tossed the comment over his shoulder, clearly sensing her hesitation.

"It was a long time ago." She tried to laugh at herself for her silly fears, but the fears hadn't diminished with age, and her laugh came out sounding forced.

"Reckon the stuff from long ago ends up haunting a person the most."

Her thoughts traveled back to that fateful day when she'd been riding one of the mares alongside their wagon train.

"It had been a particularly exhausting day of walking, so Father had let me and Scarlet take turns riding our one mare."

At her words, Maverick halted and turned so that he was giving her his full attention.

At nine, Hazel had already been a talented rider, and no one had thought anything of her wandering away for a short while to explore or to chase after a wild animal. She never went far or stayed away long.

"That evening as we started preparing to make camp, I spotted what I'd hoped was a buffalo on a nearby ridge. By the time I reached the area and realized it was just a boulder, I turned around and the wagon train wasn't in sight."

"You couldn't find your way back?"

"I probably could have, but the mare got spooked by a rattlesnake and took off so fast that it was all I could do to hang on."

Maverick's features were rugged and handsome, and the blue of his eyes was bright with an intensity that told her he was upset for her.

"By the time I got control of the mare, I was hopelessly lost. I rode for hours, well into the night, searching for everyone and calling out for them. But I didn't see a single person."

"You must have been terrified."

The horror of that night made her shiver. "I've never

felt more alone or afraid than during those hours. I thought for sure I'd be lost forever and end up dying in the plains."

"Valid concern. It was a mighty dangerous time to be traveling west."

She'd heard the tales of vigilantes wandering the West—mainly war criminals who preyed upon unsuspecting travelers. There had still been ongoing wars and hostilities with the Natives. And the wild creatures of the plains were a constant threat too.

"By dawn, I knew I had to keep going, even though I was hungry and thirsty and miserable from so many hours in the saddle. I could thankfully tell directions, and so I turned my horse toward the west and figured I'd keep riding until I reached Colorado or died, whichever came first."

Maverick muttered angry words under his breath.

"I only rode for a short while before I saw a fellow from our wagon train out riding. He was part of a large group that had set out at dawn to look for me."

"So how far away was the wagon train?"

"Not all that far, actually. Maybe half a mile or so to the southeast."

"With them being so close, they should've found you sooner."

"In all the busyness of setting up camp, they didn't realize I was missing until well after dark. By then, the leader of our group made the decision that the search party would have to wait until morning to head out."

"And leave a little girl to fend for herself all night?"

"I understand the reasoning. He didn't want one loss to turn into more, which could have easily happened in the dark."

"Don't matter none. I would've gone after you." Maverick's tone was defiant.

She smiled. "Apparently Sterling tried to go, but my father tied him up to keep him from being reckless."

"Reckon that's my downfall. I act first, think later."

"That's because you have such a big, caring heart."

"Or I'm an idiot, like Sterling said at the wedding."

"No, Maverick." She had an intense longing to reach for him and draw him into an embrace. But after the strain of the past week, she had to be careful. "He was just angry, didn't understand anything that was really going on. I was angry too, until I had more time to think about it and talk with you."

Maverick shifted and peered around again, his body tense. They'd stayed near the river, but with the banks gradually having grown steeper, Maverick had led them a dozen or more paces away—close enough to hear the rustling water, but far enough that they wouldn't chance slipping off the edge.

"You want to do what's right," she continued, "but it doesn't always work out. A few failures along the way don't mean you should stop being you."

"Those failures are mighty big ones."

"Think about all the times when your decisions have turned into something great. Like the new Oakley breed. We wouldn't have that if not for your urging and planning."

Before Maverick could answer, a frightened whinny from nearby made them both swivel and start forward.

"It's her." Hazel scanned the brush, her pulse racing forward.

As Maverick had predicted, they only had to go around a slight bend before finding the mare grazing in a secluded and shaded area beneath several fir trees at the base of a rocky slope rising gradually to the mountains beyond.

From the tautness of the mare's abdomen, Hazel guessed she was well into her travail.

As they approached, the mare nickered and tossed her head, as if warning them to stay away. But Hazel crooned gentle words of affirmation, trying to silently communicate that she didn't intend to leave, that she was a friend, and that she'd be with her for every step of the birthing.

Maverick held back, aware that the mare was unstable and needed to be handled carefully so that she didn't bolt again, this time harming herself and the unborn foal. He waited patiently to the side until at last Candy lay down.

As soon as she did, the water broke and one of the foal's front feet made an appearance.

Relief pulsed through Hazel. "That's my girl."

She smiled at Maverick over her shoulder. "It'll all work out, Maverick. Just wait and see."

He smiled in return, giving her a brief glimpse into his eyes and revealing something there that was so sweet and tender that her breath snagged.

She couldn't be sure what it was, couldn't take the time to analyze it. All she could do was pray that everything really would work out, especially between her and Maverick.

14

He loved Hazel so much it hurt.

As much as he'd tried not to love her over the past week, the feelings had only grown instead of diminishing. And being with her at another foaling made it all the harder to do what he knew he needed to—keep his distance.

He'd told Sterling he'd stay away from Hazel, that he wouldn't go near her, that he'd sacrifice his own selfish needs.

But as she knelt at Candy's head and stroked her forelock, Maverick couldn't keep from hungrily taking her in—every gentle movement, every comb of her fingers, every bend of her supple body.

"You're doing great, sweet love," Hazel said softly, trying to comfort Candy, now trembling with both fear and pain. "Almost done."

The horse whinnied, as if telling Hazel something in return.

Hazel bent in and pressed a kiss to the creature's cheek.

Maverick homed in on Hazel's lips, the hunger only pulsing deeper inside, awakening the need to kiss her— which he was finding was all too easy to awaken.

This woman was amazing. She was more than amazing. She was everything to him.

He pressed a hand over his heart. He'd never believed a heart could feel so much joy and pain or love and sorrow at the same time. But here he was, battling more emotion than he knew what to do with.

As Candy strained one last time, the foal finally slipped into the grass. Though it had dark hair, Maverick guessed it would gradually lighten and spots would develop just like the other Oakleys.

Giving the mare a final stroke, Hazel rose. She'd tossed aside her hat, or perhaps the branches of the tree had knocked it loose. Whatever the case, he loved seeing her fair hair and her pretty face more clearly.

She checked the foal, but with everything progressing now as it should, she glanced around as though looking for him, clearly having blocked him out while working— which was as it should be.

Now her gaze landed on him where he was leaning against a boulder in the shade. Her smile widened, and she started to cross to him, her bronze eyes so light they were almost gold. "She just needed encouragement. That's all."

"Reckoned she needed your soothing presence too."

Hazel didn't stop when she reached him. Instead she leaned into him and wrapped her arms around him, squeezing him tightly with her excitement.

Excitement. That's all it was. She was happy at the outcome of another foaling. She was relieved she'd made it in time to help Candy. And she was trying to share this moment with him . . . as friends.

Somehow, even though he gave himself the mental rebuke, his body didn't get the message. It reacted with a surge of desire all its own. His arms came right up to surround her. One hand slipped to the small of her back and flattened there. The other rose to the back of her neck, to the messy knot of her hair.

As he let the loose strands slip through his fingers, he almost groaned. Instead, he bent and kissed her hair, feeling the silk against his lips and drawing in a floral scent. Hopefully, the kiss would distract him from his longing for more.

But as his lips lingered, desire only swelled all the more.

His arms tightened around her, and he pressed another kiss to her head, this one harder and longer.

Her breathing stilled as though she sensed the change in him.

How could she not? Not when he radiated such intensity for her.

He shifted and kissed her temple. But the moment he tasted of her skin, he was suddenly famished and needed more of her. He kissed her forehead. Then he dropped to her cheek.

Every tiny kiss was like getting a little bit of heaven itself.

As his lips brushed at the spot beside her mouth, near her chin, he could hear her drag in a choppy breath, as if she was trying to breathe but couldn't.

The plain truth was, he'd stopped breathing the moment she'd leaned in and wrapped her arms around him.

Heaven almighty. He desperately wanted to kiss her lips again, wanted to show her how much he adored her. But with bent head, he forced himself to hold still, his cheek against hers.

"Maverick?" Her whisper near his ear was filled with a hundred questions. Questions about his reaction to her, about them, about what his intentions were, about how he felt, about how she should proceed . . .

Even though she didn't ask a single one, he could sense her confusion, especially after the past week, and he didn't want to make her more confused. But he couldn't stop himself from giving her another kiss, this one against her ear.

All of the emotion swirling through his chest swelled with such force he couldn't hold back. "I love you." The words tumbled out in a whisper so soft he wasn't sure he'd even said them.

But at her rapid intake of breath, he guessed he had.

He closed his eyes. Blast it all. What was he doing?

He was overstepping the line Sterling had drawn, that's what. Not only was he overstepping it, he'd leaped right over it and was strolling around in forbidden territory like he planned to stay and live there.

Even without his vow to Sterling to consider, he couldn't just go around telling Hazel he loved her when he'd only recently figured out his feelings. It didn't matter that he'd probably loved her for years. He was moving too fast for himself, not to mention he'd probably scared her.

He released her and took a rapid step away.

She didn't move—was frozen to the spot.

He couldn't look at her, didn't want to see her reaction to his declaration. What was she thinking? Was she afraid? More confused? Maybe she didn't return his love and didn't know how to let him down nicely.

And what would happen when Sterling learned about the declaration of love to Hazel? Because somehow Sterling seemed to find out everything.

Maverick pinched the back of his neck. He was the worst kind of friend. And he was no good for Hazel.

He should've waited to say something to her. Instead,

he'd pushed ahead like he always did, without thinking through the ramifications of his actions.

He could feel her eyes upon him, watching, waiting for him to explain himself. But what could he say that wouldn't make the situation worse?

With a frustrated exhale, he stalked off. He had to get away from her for just a few minutes—needed a moment of privacy where he could attempt to think clearly without the sight of her distracting him.

He stumbled on the rocky terrain but quick-like righted himself. A step later, he found his feet slipping. Before he knew what was happening, the layer of rocks and soil beneath him crumbled.

The haze in his mind fell away, and he realized too late that he'd wandered to the river's edge—a steep embankment of rocks with the river rushing twenty-five feet or more at the bottom of the slope.

He tried to scramble backward, his fingers grasping at tree roots, grass, brush—anything he could find. But his boots were already sliding down the slope.

He attempted to sit in order to halt the downward momentum, but the loose stones acted like saddle grease, and he found himself slipping and sliding with no way to stop the descent.

Several large boulders loomed ahead at the river's edge. If he didn't slow down or find a way to avoid them, he was gonna slam into them, and the impact—especially to his head—would probably kill him.

Frantically, he scanned the embankment for a way to save himself. His gaze snagged on a scraggly sage brush to one side of the boulders. Could he shift his position so that he ended up there instead?

Twisting as best he could, he threw his body in the direction of the brush. With every second, the speed of the descent increased, until at last he lost his footing altogether. His body flipped end over end, pain shooting through him.

A second later, he made impact and braced himself. Though his boots hit the boulder, his body landed against the sage brush. As his head slammed into the harsh cushion, his last conscious thought was of Hazel and how he hoped she wouldn't try to come down after him.

15

Where was Maverick? He'd been gone for too long.

Hazel stood from where she'd been kneeling and observing Candy and the foal and searched for a glimpse of him.

An osprey circled nearby, its slender body and narrow wings graceful in the wind current. It was likely fishing in the river, hovering ever lower before it dove down feet first to catch a fish in its talons.

She took in a deep breath of the cool morning air. With April slipping away, it wouldn't be long now before the days and nights turned warmer. But for now, the air still held the hint of winter, and the lingering piles of snow here and there were the reminders of how quickly the weather could change.

As she surveyed the landscape for the sight of Maverick's rugged, muscular frame, her heart hummed a new, sweet melody, even if it was skipping a beat with nervousness. All because Maverick had told her he loved her.

The words had been so soft but so clear that she'd known she wasn't dreaming or misunderstanding him.

He loved her.

At a shiver of anticipation, she wrapped her arms across her middle and hugged herself. She didn't have to ask him to clarify if he loved her as a friend or a woman. From the way he'd kissed her face, he'd left her with no doubt that he desired her as a woman every bit as much today as he had that night he'd first kissed her.

Even so, she still wasn't certain what he wanted. He hadn't necessarily seemed pleased with himself after telling her, almost as if he hadn't meant to and it had just slipped out.

His hesitancy could mean a number of things. Maybe he'd wanted to talk to her first before telling her of his love. Maybe he wanted to make sure she reciprocated. And though she'd never allowed herself to think of loving Maverick, she knew deep inside that she did.

On the other hand, what if his hesitancy was because he wasn't ready to be in a relationship? Especially because he was still working through his pa's death. It was possible he wanted to wait until he had the chance to put some of the pain behind him.

Whatever the case, his soft, sweet words had gone straight to her heart and filled her with the need to be with him. She didn't want to be away from him, even now. She physically felt as though a part of her was missing.

If she was completely honest, she'd always wanted to be with him, always felt complete, happier, contented when she was with him. Now that she knew he loved her, she longed to be with him even more, as if the words had given her permission to acknowledge everything she'd been trying hard to deny.

But of course, she would have to be careful. If he wasn't fully ready to embrace his love for her, she'd have to control her enthusiasm. She'd been patient for years already, hadn't she? She could continue to be patient as long as he needed.

She scanned the landscape again and guessed he'd been gone for at least thirty minutes. His gelding was still tied to one of the nearby trees, which meant if he was on foot, he probably hadn't gone far. If he needed the time to think and process this new direction of their relationship, then she couldn't be pushy and demand that he stay with her.

But what about the horse thieves? After facing the danger with his pa earlier in the year, no doubt he was concerned that the thieves were now back in the area. Since they hadn't been caught, it was very possible they'd decided to steal from High C Ranch again.

Her pulse slammed to a sudden halt.

What if Maverick had gotten into an altercation with the thieves? He might even be lying somewhere injured. Even though she hadn't heard any gunshots, there were plenty of other ways they could have harmed him. She only had to think of the tragic avalanche that had taken Mr. Oakley's life to know the truth of that.

With her heart beating again, but at double the speed, she started around the boulder in the direction Maverick had gone. It led to the river, and as she stepped closer, the rushing grew louder.

Finally she halted several feet from the bank, which was a sharp rocky drop down to the river. She glanced upstream along the ledge, but it was mostly untraversable with prickly sage plants and an uneven rim.

Downstream was a little smoother. What if he'd descended to the river? Maybe there was a trail that led safely down the steep bank, one he'd used in his childhood for fishing with Sterling. It wouldn't surprise her if the two had long ago made a path.

She inched nearer to the edge but halted at a place where it appeared the earth had given way. Was this the trail?

She knelt and then peered over, scanning the river bottom below for any sign of Maverick. She guessed he'd have a makeshift fishing pole in hand and would be standing on a boulder in the middle of the river, throwing out his line just like he used to do.

But as far as she could scan upstream and down, she didn't spot his handsome face or broad back and shoulders.

With a sigh, she began to push herself back up, but at the sight of a man lying at an odd angle almost directly below, her heart caught in her throat.

Though she couldn't view the man's head, she could see that the clothing and boots and hard muscular body belonged to only one man: Maverick.

How had he gotten there? Had he fallen?

On her knees, she cupped her hands around her mouth. "Maverick?" The shout echoed in the barren river valley enough that anyone nearby would have heard her, including Maverick.

But he didn't budge.

What if he was dead?

"Dear God, help us." Her heart began to thud with a terrible rhythm, the sweet melody from moments ago replaced with a clanging death knell.

With trembling fingers she grasped the tall grass behind her. The slight movement sent a cascade of rocks and dust down the slope, and she scrambled back to avoid falling down the embankment herself.

Was that what had happened to Maverick? Had he stepped too close to the edge and slid down? The messy cascade of rocks certainly looked like it had recently been disturbed.

Whatever the case, she had to get to him. If he was still alive, he was likely severely injured with fractured bones, cuts, internal injuries, maybe a concussion.

With growing franticness, she crawled along the embankment, searching for a way to descend—a trail, footholds, even an area that was less steep. But as far as she could tell, there was no easy way—at least, not in the near vicinity.

If she tried climbing down, she'd end up in the same shape or worse. Besides, even if she made it to him, how would she be able to help him? She only had the few supplies she'd packed just in case Candy had ended up in trouble, but none would be of use to him. She'd also never be able to move him by herself. Not back up the steep embankment, not even downriver to a different place to climb out of the river bottoms.

Her heart thudded harder. She didn't want to leave him here by himself, but the only thing left to do was go back to High C Ranch for help. Actually, she was closer to her own family's ranch and could probably reach it more quickly. Since the Noble Ranch was a bigger operation with more workers, she'd also have the likelihood of rounding up a larger rescue party.

"Maverick?" she shouted again.

He remained unmoving—didn't even twitch.

"I'm going for help!" Her voice caught on the edge of a sob. "I'll be back in no time." At least, she prayed she would be.

She waited only a second longer, praying he'd sit up or lift a hand or at least shift his leg. But he was as silent as a dead man.

A sob slipped out, echoing in the eerily silent air. She crept backward. When she was safely away from the ledge, she stood and ran back to Candy and the foal. The two were still right where she'd left them and would be fine while she was gone.

And Maverick's gelding was still tied up and grazing peacefully.

His horse.

No. She shook her head. She couldn't ride his horse.

She'd run all the way to the ranch as fast as she could . . . it wouldn't take her long. She guessed she had only a mile or so left at the most. It wasn't far. She could make it easily enough.

But even as she scanned the rocky terrain ahead, sobs clawed against her chest and several more broke free.

"I love him too." She forced her feet toward the gelding, tears rolling down her cheeks. When she reached the lead line, she didn't hesitate to unwind it, even though her hands trembled so much that she could hardly make them work.

She led the gelding out from under the tree. With tears blurring her vision and sobs choking her, she stuck her foot into the stirrup. Then with shaking legs, she climbed up and into the saddle.

As she situated herself, nausea rose swiftly. She bent over the side of the horse and retched, not sure what she detested more—leaving Maverick behind or riding the horse.

But she didn't have a choice if she had any hope of saving Maverick. She had to ride as fast as she possibly could for help. There was no other option.

She tapped her heels into the gelding's thighs, nudged it with a shake of the reins, and then clung tightly to the pommel. As the horse began to trot forward, another swell of nausea rose, but she swallowed it, not wanting to waste another moment—not when Maverick's life might depend on it.

Tears clouded her vision, but thankfully the gelding had been in Dead Man's Gulch enough over the years to be familiar with the path that led to the Noble Ranch. When she finally crossed the bridge that spanned the Blue River and the south pasture came into view, her sobs came again. This time uncontrollably.

She loved Maverick more than anything or anyone. If he died, she didn't know how she'd be able to go on without him. She had to save him, had to find a way to get a rescue party out to him immediately.

She scanned the pastures and the barns beyond, searching for anyone who could ride back with her, praying all the ranch hands weren't out with the livestock far away. At the sight of several men in a corral next to the barn, her heart kicked at her ribs to go faster. She dug in her heels, lowered herself, and flew across the final distance of the pasture.

As she did so, she realized she was no longer afraid to be on Maverick's gelding. In fact, she wasn't afraid of the horse at all. She was grateful to have it, to be able to ride so swiftly, to have the creature so intuitive to her need to help Maverick—because she had no doubt the gelding understood that something had happened and felt the urgency to intervene.

A tall fellow in the corral stepped away from the others to watch her approach. It took her only a second to recognize Sterling's imposing build and the confident way he held himself.

She could tell the moment he realized she was on the horse when he hopped the fence in one easy motion and began to jog toward her.

As she drew nearer, she tried to rein in her sobs, but the tears kept slipping down her cheeks.

"What happened?" Sterling's shout was filled with worry and his face taut with fear.

He, along with all her family, knew that she'd refused to mount a horse since that night she'd been lost. He and all her family understood how petrified she was of riding alone. He and all her family had gotten frustrated at her for her stubbornness in not riding because of the inconvenience it was at times.

Now to see her on a horse, galloping wildly? He had to have realized something was very wrong.

She reined in and the bile began to work its way back up her throat. "It's Maverick. He's hurt."

Sterling stumbled to a halt, his body turning suddenly rigid.

In her rush to get Maverick help, she'd forgotten all about Sterling's and Maverick's falling-out. What if Sterling refused to help Maverick because of his anger and unforgiveness? She couldn't let that happen. She had to make Sterling see reason.

"Maverick isn't to blame for what happened, Sterling." Her voice came out too forcefully. She wasn't normally given to shouting or brazen displays. That was Scarlet's forte.

But in this moment, with Maverick lying along the river, his body broken, his life ebbing from him—if not already gone—she couldn't be gentle and patient with Sterling any longer.

"Everyone but you knows the truth," she said through her sniffles. "Violet never loved you as much as you loved her, and she wasn't ready for marriage."

Sterling took a small step back as though her words had punched him in the gut.

"She was already getting ready to run off when Maverick saw her outside. He knew it. And so, because he cared about you, he scooped her up and tried to take her back inside the house."

Beneath the brim of Sterling's hat, his sun-browned face had turned pale—or as pale as it could get. He pressed his lips together, the sure sign he was holding back his anger.

"She kissed Maverick to sabotage the wedding. I know you don't want to hear this, Sterling, but it's the truth."

He remained silent, but from the slight hunch of his shoulders, Hazel guessed he'd already been arriving at his own similar conclusions.

"Maverick took the blame because he was hoping to save your relationship with Violet. He figured if you thought he was at fault, you wouldn't be so upset at Violet."

Sterling's shoulders slumped even further.

"Now Maverick is out there hurt badly." This time her words broke with a sob. "And you have to put aside your issues and go help him."

Sterling opened his mouth to speak.

Before he could deny her, she forced the rest of what she had to say out. "If you don't forgive him and do this, you'll have to live with knowing you killed your best friend. Is that what you want?"

"I'll go, Hazel. You don't have to say any more."

"You'll go?"

"Maverick isn't my best friend anymore. But I won't

turn my back on someone in need, not even if they're my worst enemy."

The tears started flowing again.

"You doing okay?" His voice softened as he took her in astride the saddle.

She nodded. "I'll be okay once we get back to Maverick."

"Then you're willing to lead us to him?" Sterling's voice held compassion. After years of fear controlling her, no doubt he was finding it hard to believe she'd willingly remain on the horse.

"I'll stay on this horse all day if it will save Maverick." She was still clutching the reins tightly, her fingers aching from her grip, but somehow she knew it was less from fear of riding and more because of the urgency she was feeling for Maverick.

Sterling gave a quick nod, his eyes filling with emotion and turning glassy. Then he spun and began to jog back to the barn.

She swiped at the tears on her cheeks. Sometimes love gave a person the courage to do the impossible. And today her love for Maverick had made her braver than she'd ever been before.

She just prayed she had the strength to endure whatever outcome they found when they finally reached him.

16

The section of the river where Maverick had fallen wasn't easy to reach.

But Sterling knew the area well enough that he was able to locate another place downstream where they could descend into the river bottom and then make their way upstream, mostly by riding in the river itself.

Hazel went right along with the fellows, having no trouble making her way over the difficult terrain. Even though it had been more than a decade since she'd been in the saddle, she knew how to read horses better than almost anyone and was able to guide Maverick's horse without having to say a word.

When they reached the embankment, she pointed out his body, hidden among the rocks and brush. They found a level spot to dismount, then Sterling and the ranch hands began to climb up the steep bank toward Maverick while Hazel stayed back with their horses. Even though she wanted to rush to him and be the first to know his condition, Sterling had been insistent that she stay away from the slippery slope.

They'd brought medical supplies as well as a stretcher. Even if Maverick woke up by some miracle, he'd likely need to be transported back to the ranch and wouldn't be able to sit in a saddle. Sterling had already sent a man to fetch Dr. Howell from Breckenridge, and hopefully he'd be waiting for them at the ranch when they got there with Maverick. They'd already decided to bring him back to the Noble Ranch since it was closer.

Carefully Sterling led the way up the incline. Rocks shifted and crumbled with each step he took, but Sterling didn't stop. He pushed forward quickly until he reached Maverick.

As he knelt beside him, he gently lifted Maverick's head. From what Hazel could see, Maverick was limp and unresponsive, and her breath tightened in her chest with every passing second that she waited for Sterling's assessment.

When Sterling finally lifted his head and met her gaze across the distance, his expression held relief. "He's alive."

Hazel nodded, her own relief weakening her so that she had to hang on to the gelding to keep from sliding down into the rocks and pebbles alongside the river where she waited.

"He's breathing, and his heartbeat is steady."

Sterling's pronouncement rose above the rushing water, the most welcome news Hazel had ever heard in her life.

"Let's get that stretcher here." With a wave he beckoned his men.

Sterling seemed to know just what to do, directing the others with precise instructions for how to climb, where to lift Maverick, how to lay him on the stretcher, then how to carry him down the hill so that they didn't jostle him too much.

As soon as they were near the river, Hazel rushed to Maverick.

His eyes were closed, and his face was streaked with dust and grit and blood. He had a gash on the side of his head that was oozing blood. He also had a cut near one of his eyebrows that was bleeding and would likely need stitches. From the blood staining his trouser legs, he probably had some deep tears there too.

Sterling held one side of the stretcher and was moving carefully. "From what I can tell, he has a dislocated shoulder."

"Reckon he's got a doozy of a concussion," said one of the men.

Sterling's eyes were grave. "He's lucky he landed in the brush and didn't bash his head on the rocks."

Hazel's insides churned over how close she'd come to losing Maverick. In some ways she felt as if she'd only just started her life with him, or at least this new life where he'd stopped treating her like his friend's sister and saw her as a desirable woman.

Now that her dreams were coming true, she wanted to make the most of the time they had and didn't want to miss out on the chance to be with him. Life was too short and uncertain to let anything more come between them.

With the men having to carry Maverick, the journey back to the ranch seemed to take forever, especially because Sterling was trying not to hurt Maverick any more than he already was.

Hazel and another ranch hand led the horses on foot. And with every step she took, she was relieved not to be riding anymore.

When they made it to the house, she was surprised when Sterling directed the men to put Maverick in his room instead of one of the guest rooms. Thankfully, the doctor was already there and set to work right away tending to Maverick's injuries.

Since they had to cut Maverick out of his clothing, Sterling wouldn't allow her to be in the room. Instead, she paced the hallway, waiting for the doctor's prognosis. Scarlet and her mother waited with her.

Soon they were joined by Clementine and Tanner. Hazel was thankful Sterling had been thoughtful enough to send a messenger over to the Oakleys regarding Maverick's accident. She prayed that meant everyone was learning to forgive Maverick and moving on from

Sterling's failed wedding.

As the bedroom door finally opened, Dr. Howell and Sterling stepped out while conversing in low tones.

Hazel stopped pacing.

All eyes turned upon the doctor expectantly. An older man with a few tufts of gray hair upon his head, the doctor came to an abrupt halt at the sight of the hallway filled with so many people. Small in size—not even as tall as Hazel's petite frame—he straightened his spine, as though trying to give himself an extra inch.

"Well, doctor?" Clementine spoke first, her pretty face lined with worry. No doubt she was dreading losing someone else she loved.

With a solemn gaze, the doctor cleared his throat. He started to speak, then stopped to clear his throat again.

Hazel's heart sank. Was he trying to deliver bad news?

"I'm sorry," the doctor started as he exchanged a serious look with Sterling, who was abnormally subdued. "But Maverick is gravely injured."

"What does that mean?" Clementine asked before anyone else could.

"It appears that he may have fractured his spine." The doctor's words came out in a rush.

A pall fell over them, leaving them all speechless, including Clementine.

"We won't know until he awakens," the doctor continued solemnly, "but it appears that he has no movement in his lower extremities."

Hazel tried to make sense of the doctor's news, but she couldn't seem to think or breathe.

"Then he's paralyzed?" Tanner asked.

The doctor's frail shoulders fell, and again he cleared his throat. "I'm afraid it's a possibility."

Maverick paralyzed? Hazel couldn't begin to imagine how he would handle never being able to walk again. He'd be devastated. With as much life and energy as Maverick always had, he'd likely feel that his life was over.

"How much of his body is still functional?" Tanner persisted.

"Again, I can't be sure." The doctor glanced through the open bedroom door, where only the footboard of the bed was visible. "I do believe he'll have motion in his arms and hands. But time will tell."

The ache in Hazel's chest pulsed through her body. How would Maverick be able to function? And who would take care of him?

Clementine's forehead was creased. She was likely thinking that they were busy with their ailing mother, and how would they be able to tend to Maverick too?

Clementine exchanged a look with Tanner. "We'll go back for the wagon and transport him home."

Tanner nodded, running his fingers through his overlong brown hair that was curling at the nape of his neck.

"No," Sterling said, his tone firm. "The doctor thinks the less Maverick is moved around, the better chance he'll have at recovery."

"It'll be fine." Tanner spoke curtly, turning cold eyes on Sterling. "After all the traveling he's already done, a little more won't harm him. Besides, he'll want to be someplace where he's welcome."

Hazel's gaze bounced back and forth between Tanner and Sterling. Tanner was obviously upset that Sterling had blamed Maverick for Violet calling off the wedding. And he didn't want to leave Maverick behind in what he considered a hostile place.

Sterling held Tanner's gaze. "He's welcome here." It was as close to an apology as Sterling would give. Hopefully Tanner realized that.

Tanner hesitated and slid a glance at Hazel, his brows rising as if to ask her opinion.

"I'll tend to Maverick." The moment her offer was out for everyone to analyze, embarrassment swept through her. "I mean, I'm sure between the maids and us women folk"—she waved a hand at her mother and Scarlet—"we'll be able to take good care of Maverick, especially since Clementine and Clarabelle need to be with Mrs. Oakley."

Thankfully, her mother nodded. "Of course we can all help."

Hazel had always been told that she looked like a

younger version of her mother, having the same blond hair and bronze eyes and delicate features. More than outward beauty, her mother had an inner gentleness and politeness that Hazel had always admired and strove to imitate. Now was one of those times she was relieved that her mother was so gracious.

Scarlet, on the other hand, was scowling and shaking her head. She had fair hair too, but her eyes were a vibrant blue and were always so expressive, never leaving any doubt regarding her true feelings. Even though she'd been worried about Maverick, she wasn't ready to forgive him for the way he'd hurt Sterling, and she certainly didn't want to take care of him.

"No," Scarlet whispered to Mother. "He can't stay."

Mother slipped an arm around Scarlet's waist and began to lead her down the hallway toward the stairs. Hazel was grateful for Mother's intervention so that they didn't have to deal with one of Scarlet's tantrums.

Tanner wasn't paying attention to Scarlet or Mother. Instead, his gaze was squarely upon Hazel. "We don't want to impose on you, Hazel."

"It's the least I can do." Her voice wobbled with all the emotion she'd yet to sort through. "I'm the one who dragged him out to find Candy."

"You're not to blame." Tanner's tone was soothing, as if he were talking to an easily spooked mare. "I should have gone out with you."

Deep inside, she knew Maverick's accident wasn't her fault any more than it was Tanner's. Even so, finding someone to blame—including oneself—always seemed to be the natural way of reacting to a tragedy.

She swallowed the lump in her throat that threatened to push up and make her start crying again. She'd already shed enough tears for one day and had to stay strong. "I'll be a good nurse. You won't have to worry about Maverick."

Tanner studied her a heartbeat longer, as though trying to determine her innermost thoughts. When he finally nodded, his mind made up, she sagged against the wall, grateful that she wouldn't have to be away from Maverick.

"I was planning to head out today," Tanner said, "but I'll stay and help at the ranch until Maverick is able to come home and resume his duties."

If Maverick ever reached the point where he could work again. But of course, she didn't voice her thought aloud.

She'd stay home and take care of Maverick as long as it took. Forever if need be. "I may need to cut back on how much time I can spend with the mares."

Tanner waved off her concern. "I'll manage."

"But the foalings—"

"I'll send you word if one of the mares goes into labor."

She hesitated. After Candy's foaling, she had at least a week, if not more, before the next mare was due. "I'll come over when I can to check on things."

"Don't worry about anything." Clementine squeezed her arm. "Clarabelle and I will be there to help."

Hazel waited for Sterling to object to the unfolding plans, but he stood quietly beside the doctor, his shoulders slumped, his eyes sad.

Knowing Sterling and how sensitive he was beneath all his bluster and brawn, she guessed he was having regrets about the way his relationship with Maverick had deteriorated, especially how he'd harbored such anger and unforgiveness instead of at least treating Maverick with some civility.

Even though she hated that Maverick had experienced the accident and would suffer as a result, she could only pray it would bring about healing, especially to their hearts.

17

Maverick shifted and then groaned. Every bone in his body felt like it had been jerked out of joint and every inch of flesh bruised.

A soft hand smoothed back his hair on his forehead, followed by a gentle press of lips. Hazel's hands and lips.

He breathed in the floral scent that sometimes lingered in her hair, suddenly needing her more than life.

She seemed to be leaning into him, her body slightly pressed against his chest. And in the next moment, she brushed another kiss to his face, this one to his cheek.

"Am I dreaming?" he murmured.

She drew in a sharp breath. "Maverick? Are you awake?"

He cracked open his eyes to find that he was in bed and she was sitting on the edge of the bed, bent over him.

"Hey, angel." His voice was groggy, and his smile felt weak.

Her beautiful eyes welled with sudden tears, and before he knew what was happening, she leaned down and touched her lips to his.

No way he was complaining about waking up to one of her kisses. No way, no how. He didn't know why he was in bed or why she was at his side or why she was so emotional. All that mattered was that she was kissing him.

Her lips plied at his tenderly, as if she might break him if she pressed too hard. Her mouth teased his with the phantom of a kiss, not even the real thing. Even so, the touch of her lips, of her chest against his, of her fingers still in his hair—it awakened him from what felt like a deep slumber, and suddenly he was alert and alive and aware of need pulsing in his blood.

Swift longing surged through him—a longing for her that was sharp and keen and greater than anything else. Before she could end the kiss, he lifted his head and took possession of her lips, devouring her mouth as though he wouldn't ever get enough . . . because the truth was, he never would, not even if he kissed her every day for the rest of his life.

She didn't pull away. Instead she seemed to be greedily consuming him in return, her lips melding and molding against his with a desperation he didn't quite understand.

But he didn't need to understand anything except that Hazel was his. He'd laid claim to her, and she hadn't resisted. Instead, she'd capitulated as if she'd been waiting for him and now wanted him forever.

That wasn't really possible. They'd grown up together. She was younger. And she'd always been off-limits . . . because she was Sterling's sister.

Sterling.

He broke the kiss and pulled back.

She hovered above him, only an inch away, her ragged breathing bathing his mouth and tempting him to snag her lips into another kiss and another and another.

His own breathing was shallow, and with her beautiful face above his and her honey-brown eyes peering down at him, he didn't know why it should matter that she was Sterling's sister, especially since she was so grown-up and mature.

"How are you feeling?" Both hands were on his face, on his cheeks, on his jaw, then back in his hair.

Her touch was so amazing that he closed his eyes to simply enjoy the sensation. "I'd feel better if you were kissing me again," he whispered.

She didn't respond and didn't bend in the way he'd hoped she would.

As he opened his eyes, he found her still only inches away. Her fair hair was in a single braid with a few loose strands surrounding her pretty face—the lines so elegant and so soft at the same time.

Heaven almighty. She was exquisite. In fact, he

couldn't imagine anything else in all of creation that could compare to her.

"Do you remember what happened?" she whispered.

His gaze got stuck on her lips, so full and softly rounded. Just another small kiss wouldn't hurt anything, would it?

She moved back, still partially lying on him but far enough away that he couldn't so easily kiss her again. Her fingers glided from his hair down to his cheeks again, grazing his scruff as if she couldn't get enough of the feel of him. "You were in an accident."

"An accident?" His mind scrambled to make sense of what she was saying.

Her hands stilled. "Yes, you fell down an embankment, cut yourself up badly, dislocated your shoulder, and have been unconscious all day."

At her words, everything tumbled back into his memory. They'd gone after Candy, he'd gone too close to the edge of the river, and he'd slipped in the rocks and hadn't been able to catch himself.

He was suddenly aware of the pain that was shooting through his head, back, ribs, shoulder, arms . . . everything except his legs. In fact, he felt nothing in the lower half of his body. As he tried to shift his foot, he had the odd sensation that he didn't even have feet anymore.

With a surge of panic mixed with determination, he struggled to push himself up.

"No, Maverick." She tried to hold him in place. "You shouldn't move. The doctor thinks you may have fractured your spine during the fall."

He shrugged off her hold. Though his arms were weak, he made it to his elbows. Then, with a burst of desperation, he struggled the rest of the way until he was sitting.

Hazel was perched on the edge of the bed. The glow of a lantern on the bedside table revealed the worry filling her eyes.

Excruciating pain radiated up and down his spine. He didn't think it was broken, but he'd definitely injured it. Had he permanently lost movement in his legs as a result?

He shifted again, and the pain—especially in his tailbone—nearly made him cry out.

"You've got to take it easy," she chided softly. "You don't want to make things worse."

He'd watched many a man over his lifetime pick himself back up after getting injured, particularly his pa. There had even been the time when his pa had gotten bucked from a stallion and thrown into a pile of hay, where a pitchfork had impaled his leg. They'd still been living in Kentucky on the horse farm, and he'd been just a little tyke. But he'd never forgotten how his pa had stood up, pulled out the pitchfork, and limped away, even with blood saturating his trousers.

Through that example and plenty of others, his pa

had taught him to expect the hardships and not to run from the pain. The true test of strength wasn't whether a man could endure. Instead it was in how strong he could grow as a result of battling the pain.

Maverick ground his teeth together, then swiveled on the bed. His legs shifted only slightly, but it was enough to tell him that he hadn't lost their use altogether.

Hazel stood, obviously sensing he wouldn't be persuaded to stay still. She knew he'd never let himself be confined to a bed. At least, not for long.

Even so, her pretty face was lined with worry. "Be careful, Maverick."

He wasn't about to be careful. He was determined to get on his feet, and he didn't care if he had to do so by sheer willpower alone—he was gonna do it. Summoning all his strength, he slowly began to move his legs, one small increment at a time. When he finally had them near the edge of the bed, the pain in his back was so intense he was dizzy. But he forced himself to keep shifting, dropping first one leg to the floor, then the next.

He wasn't in his clothes, was instead wearing a light cotton shirt and underdrawers. He reckoned his clothing had been ripped and bloodstained, maybe even past repairing. Regardless of his scantily clad state, he had to prove to himself that he would get better, that he wouldn't let the accident hold him down.

As he settled his feet against the braided rug that

covered the wood floor, he paused at the sight of the colorful strands, then he glanced around, taking in the spacious room that belonged to Sterling. Why was he in the Nobles' house and in Sterling's room, especially since Sterling hated him?

It didn't matter. He gave himself a mental shake and forced himself to concentrate on each tiny movement. He could hardly feel the rug beneath his toes, but he shoved himself up from the bed, wobbling like a newborn foal first standing.

Hazel hovered by his side, her hand out to catch him if he faltered. But she understood him enough to let him attempt to stand on his own without her help.

The pressure on his tailbone, though, was excruciating. Even though his legs were numb, he could feel his muscles spasming.

Before he could grab onto anything or even lower himself back to the bed, he felt himself going down. His knees buckled and his legs folded, dropping him heavily to his knees on the floor.

Hazel released a startled cry just as he cried out at the pain. It wasn't a loud holler, but he hated the weakness in himself and clamped his jaw closed.

In the next instant, Hazel was kneeling beside him, grasping his arm. "Are you all right?"

He couldn't speak past the pain.

"Let me help you back into bed," Hazel quietly urged.

He shook his head.

Heavy footfalls sounded on the stairway and then slapped the hallway floor. Maverick didn't have to wonder who the steps belonged to. They were familiar enough from years of hearing them.

A moment later, Sterling burst through the open door into the room. His face was scruffy, his clothing dusty, and a hat ring matted his hair. From not only his presence in the house but the darkness out the window, it was probably the supper hour.

Maverick drew in a steadying breath. No doubt Sterling had been out in one of the pastures and hadn't known about the accident. Hazel, being the sweet woman that she was, had brought him up to the room intending to help but hadn't given thought to what Sterling would think about taking over the bedroom.

Sterling swept his gaze from the bed to Maverick to Hazel and back.

Maverick's gut tightened, and he braced himself for Sterling's wrath—at the very least a cold voice demanding that he leave.

Sterling had told him to stay away from Hazel. Now here he was in a bedroom alone with her. He was wearing only his undergarments. And he'd kissed her while he'd been lying in Sterling's bed. Even if he didn't say anything to Sterling, the fellow would figure out his transgressions. No doubt the guilt was written all over his face.

"What are you doing?" Sterling's brows furrowed.

"Don't worry." Maverick gripped the edge of the bed and began to pull himself back up. "I'm leaving just as soon as I can manage it."

"Leaving?" Sterling's tone took on a scoffing note, and he began to cross to Maverick. "Really? You think so?"

"Yep." Maverick hoisted himself up so that he was hunched over, then he grabbed the headboard for support. "I didn't know Hazel brought me here." He could hardly see straight through the wave of pain, and perspiration broke out on his forehead.

"She didn't bring you here." Sterling was at his side in the next instant and was slipping an arm around his waist and bracing him up. "I did."

Maverick froze.

Sterling nudged him back toward the bed.

Maverick couldn't get his feet to work and would have collapsed again if not for Sterling's arm supporting him.

"If you don't get back in bed, I'll put you there myself." Sterling's voice came out a low growl, but it held a hint of humor.

What was going on?

Maverick didn't resist as Sterling helped him climb

into bed. He was in too much pain to talk and had to use every ounce of concentration to get his legs working again.

When he was finally lying down, he was breathing hard from the exertion, and he had to close his eyes to fight against the pain and exhaustion.

He could feel Sterling's presence at the side of the bed and Hazel's at the end. Both were watching him.

"I'll go home tomorrow," Maverick managed to say.

Sterling pressed against his shoulder as if to keep him in place. "No, you'll stay here. It's already been decided."

Maverick pried his eyes open and found himself peering up at Sterling. "I can't impose. Know you don't want me here—"

"I want you here." Sterling's expression turned earnest. "I want you to stay until you can get around on your own again."

Maverick shook his head. He hadn't been paralyzed. Thank the good Lord for that. But he was gonna have a long road to recovery, and the last thing he wanted was Sterling feeling sorry for him. "I'll be up and moving in no time."

"Hazel's sticking close to home so that she can help take care of you."

Maverick didn't dare look at her. "I'm not imposing on Hazel either."

"You won't be, Maverick," she rushed to say. "Tanner

said he'd stay on at the ranch and take care of things until you're back."

He was having a hard time believing Sterling was okay with the plans. Not after how angry his friend had been.

Sterling stuffed his hands into his pockets and trained his gaze on the dark window. "I owe you an apology, Maverick."

As uncomfortable as Maverick was, Sterling's words brought the tumult inside his chest and head to a standstill.

Sterling continued to stare out the window, his Adam's apple bobbing up then down. "I was wrong to accuse you of ruining my wedding."

"I should've been more careful—"

"It was all Violet's fault." Sterling's gaze fell back on Maverick.

He wanted to deny Sterling's statement, but it was the truth, and the heartache in his friend's eyes told him that Sterling had finally accepted the truth too.

"Even if you'd been at fault," Sterling said quietly, "I shouldn't have reacted the way I did."

"I understand. I shouldn't have kissed her back."

"That's just it." Sterling's voice wavered with emotion. "You're the kind of friend who's willing to take the blame for something you didn't do in order to spare my feelings."

Had Hazel told Sterling what really happened the

morning of the wedding?

She wouldn't meet his gaze and instead fidgeted with tucking the blanket into the end of the mattress more securely.

"You've always been a good friend and a good man, Maverick." Again Sterling's words were tinged with heavy emotion. "I couldn't ask for a better friend."

A lump pushed up into Maverick's throat.

"I just hope you can forgive me for throwing our friendship aside instead of working things out man to man."

Maverick swallowed hard. "Course I forgive you. Hope you can forgive me too."

"Nothin' to forgive."

That wasn't exactly true. Guilt pricked at Maverick sharply. He'd betrayed Sterling by letting his feelings for Hazel run out of control. Even if Sterling had told him to stay away from Hazel partly out of his frustration and anger, Maverick had agreed to it. And instead of being a man of his word, he'd let his attraction to Hazel get the best of him. He'd even told her he loved her. That's what had sent him running from her out by the river and caused his accident to begin with.

To make matters worse, he'd just kissed her right in this room in Sterling's bed. If that wasn't disloyalty to his friend, he didn't know what was.

An apology swelled within Maverick. He needed to

confess what he'd done. Yet how could he? Now that he'd reached a tenuous truce with Sterling, he'd only make his friend angry all over again, and he didn't want to do that.

Sterling hesitated at his bedside a moment longer before turning and crossing the room. He paused in the door. "Glad you're here, Mav. Realized mighty fast today that I don't want to lose you too."

With that, Sterling ducked out of the room.

Maverick's chest pinched tighter with more guilt. As Hazel moved back to the side of his bed and gently squeezed his arm, he closed his eyes and fought against his need for her.

Sterling had offered him the hand of friendship. If he went behind Sterling's back and continued to let his relationship with Hazel grow, then he'd hurt and betray his friend again.

For the time being, he couldn't do anything that would jeopardize the fragile reconciliation he'd started with Sterling. That meant he'd have to put aside his feelings for Hazel. As much as he loved her and wanted her, he wouldn't go about getting her the wrong way, sneaking around behind Sterling's back to see her.

No, when the time came to start courting her, he wanted to do so properly and openly with the support of both their families. For that to happen, he was gonna need to give Sterling more time and allow their friendship to get back on solid ground first.

In the meantime, he'd have to switch back to viewing Hazel as just a friend. Doing so would be nearly impossible. He knew that. But he valued his friendship with Sterling too much to make another mistake. So even if resisting Hazel ended up being the hardest thing he'd ever done, he was gonna do it.

It was the right thing to do.

18

Maverick was a terrible patient. But Hazel loved having him at the house anyway.

She finished arranging the breakfast tray with all his favorite foods—scrambled eggs, sausage, biscuits slathered in jam, and a bowl of peaches from the last of the jars she'd helped her mother can last autumn.

As she placed the steaming mug of coffee beside the plate, she paused at the thumping of his cane and uneven steps overhead.

They'd all been relieved—including Dr. Howell when he'd come again yesterday—to learn Maverick hadn't been paralyzed. The doctor believed Maverick had pinched a nerve, which was causing the numbness and lack of mobility.

The doctor had indicated that it would take time for Maverick to heal and regain full function of his legs. He'd insisted Maverick rest and remain motionless for several more days in order for his back to heal properly.

But Maverick was disobeying the doctor's orders. Again.

Hazel pursed her lips, picked up the tray, and headed out of the kitchen.

Morning sunlight slanted through the hallway window and promised another beautiful spring day. The house was quiet and mostly deserted. Sterling was already out with his men doing chores. Mother and Scarlet were in the large vegetable garden behind the house, planting the crops that could withstand the cold and more snowfall that could still come at any time over the next month.

Although Jo-Jo was upstairs making beds and tidying rooms, Hazel hadn't asked their sweet maid for help with anything. She'd also declined assistance from her mother and Scarlet. Selfishly, she'd wanted to take care of Maverick by herself—or at least, as much as Sterling would let her.

He'd been the one to stay at Maverick's bedside during the night, attending to Maverick's personal needs at bedtime and sending Hazel away. He'd only allowed her back into the room in the morning after Maverick was dressed, groomed, and ready for the day.

She was relieved Sterling had apologized and tried to right his relationship with Maverick. Although the easygoing camaraderie between the two wasn't back yet, at least they were talking to each other again.

After Sterling left Maverick's room, she took over caring for him, and she'd gotten to spend the past two days by his bedside. While he'd slept for long hours at a time, she hadn't wanted to be anywhere else. During his waking moments, he hadn't spoken much. From the tight lines in his face and the glassiness of his eyes, she'd been able to tell he was fighting pain, even with the opium pills the doctor had given him.

To distract him, she'd set up first checkers and then backgammon, and they'd played in between his fitful bouts of sleep. But his frustration with himself and the situation had been growing.

As she started up the steps, she prayed today would be a better day, that he'd be in less pain, and that he'd start to regain more function in his legs.

And she prayed he wouldn't get frustrated with their relationship. At times he interacted with her normally, without any strange tension. But then other times, like this morning when she'd entered the room shortly after Sterling left at dawn, Maverick's gaze had landed upon her hungrily. He'd taken her in with such need she'd almost been breathless by the time she crossed to the bed.

A part of her had debated bending down and kissing him like she had when he'd regained consciousness. But he'd closed his eyes, shifted away from her, and gone back to sleep.

It was probably for the best that she hadn't kissed him

again. Because even though she'd only meant to show her relief that morning, the kiss had swiftly changed into something much more passionate.

In fact, it had shaken her, perhaps even more than his first kiss. Or maybe she'd just been reeling with how close she'd come to losing him. Whatever the case, his kisses left her with only a desire to kiss him more.

Even now, she wanted to be brave enough to walk into his room, go over to him, and let her lips touch his. Why couldn't she? No one was there to stop her. And no one would have to know, not even Jo-Jo—especially if she was quiet and closed the bedroom door.

Of course, Sterling had told her to leave the door open when she was taking care of Maverick, that he didn't want her to be alone in the bedroom with a man. Her father had reiterated the same thing last night when he'd finally come home from the silver mine and learned of Maverick's accident.

She understood the reasoning behind the rule. If she closed the door, soon enough the ranch hands would learn of it, and her reputation would suffer.

No, she wouldn't close the door. And she wouldn't kiss him again. But as she made her way quietly down the hallway toward Sterling's bedroom, her pulse picked up pace at just the thought of seeing him again . . . and because she loved him.

Yes, she truly and deeply loved him. She'd allowed

herself to acknowledge her love the day of the accident. Was it time to tell him?

He hadn't said anything more about his love. What if he was waiting to say it again until he knew how she felt? Maybe she had to be the one to make the next move.

As she stepped into the doorway, he was standing by a far chair that held the bag of his clothing Clementine had brought over. He was leaning against the wall and attempting to shrug into a coat. His movements were jerky, his muscles and limbs still not cooperating well.

"Maverick," she chided. "You shouldn't be up."

He didn't stop, just grunted as he tugged his coat up over his broad shoulders.

She placed the breakfast tray on the bureau and crossed toward him. "You don't need your coat on. If you're cold, I'll get another blanket."

"I'm not cold." His body might not be cold, but something in his tone was most definitely cold.

She halted several feet away from him. He was an independent man and didn't like to show weakness or accept help. All the Oakley men were like that—tough and single-minded.

As he finished slipping his other arm into the coat, he straightened and pushed away from the wall, holding onto his cane tightly, the muscles in his hand taut and his veins showing.

He glanced out the window, his face flushed from the

cane and rested his arm against the windowpane. He needed to get back into bed, but he was too stubborn for his own good.

"Please, Maverick, just stay a few more days and rest. It won't hurt you."

"It's killing me."

"What's killing you?"

"I need to be back at my place, all right?"

She didn't understand why that was so important to him, but she'd do her best to respect his decision. "Fine. Then I'll stay at your house and take care of you there."

He released a low, mirthless laugh. "That won't work."

"Why not? It's the perfect solution. I can stay in the loft and look out for you during the day. When you're resting, then I'll go out and spend some time with the mares."

"No."

The abruptness of his refusal was like a slap in the face. She tried to tell herself he wasn't rejecting her again like he had after their initial kiss, that this was different, but somehow it felt like she was following him down a path she didn't want to take, and she was helpless to turn back.

Maybe if he knew the truth about how she felt, he'd change his mind. "I want to be with you, Maverick." Her voice came out soft, plaintive. That night when she'd fallen asleep on him on his sofa, he'd mentioned that they ought to just get married. The idea of doing so had startled her then.

But now . . . she realized she would marry him in a heartbeat if it meant she never had to leave his side.

He was still staring out the window, his shoulders rigid.

She approached him. Maybe if she wrapped her arms around him and hugged him from behind, she'd show him how much she cared about him and wanted to be with him wherever that was.

As she stopped only inches from him, she lifted a hand, then hesitated. Something wasn't right—hadn't been right since she'd stepped into the room with his breakfast. She touched his back lightly.

He flinched and hobbled a step away.

She remained frozen to her spot, an ache forming in her chest. He was definitely pushing her away again. "I assumed you wanted to be with me too . . . after what you told me out in Dead Man's Gulch."

She willed him to respond, to turn around and tell her that he loved her again and that he'd do whatever it took to be together.

But his silence filled the air.

She hadn't been wrong about everything, had she? Surely he hadn't simply been flirting with her, telling her all the right things and leading her on with kisses because she was just another woman in his life to win over.

All of his attention had meant more than that, hadn't it?

She had to know. "Say something, Maverick."

He remained quiet for another moment, then he exhaled loudly. "We can't be together, Hazel." His voice was low but filled with determination. "Not here and not at my home."

"I don't understand." The pain in her chest was swelling. "I thought we were starting to care about each other. I thought you wanted to be with me . . . like I want to be with you."

With slumping shoulders, he dropped his head and leaned it against the window. "I'm sorry, but it won't work between us right now."

"Then someday?" If he could give her any indication of a future, she'd wait for him, just as she'd always done.

He hesitated. Then he shook his head. "I don't know."

The uncertainty was as bad as if he'd outright told her no, because obviously he didn't care about her enough to fight for her—for them—and for whatever this was that had started to develop. If he was willing to let her go so easily for a second time, then she didn't want him.

"You pushed me aside after our first kiss." The heat began to sting the backs of her eyes, but she didn't want to cry around him, didn't want him to see how much his rejection was hurting her. "Now you're pushing me away after our second."

"I didn't mean to kiss you either time."

"Oh, so kissing me both times was a mistake?" She couldn't stop the anger from swelling now too.

"I shouldn't have done it—"

"Then why did you?"

He didn't answer.

She wanted to stomp her foot and demand an answer. But she knew Maverick all too well, and she guessed he truly didn't have an answer and was as confused by everything that had transpired between them as she was.

At the rattle of a wagon on the lane that led to the house, she guessed Tanner was coming.

She took a step back, the anger already dispersing inside her. She never had been able to stay frustrated at Maverick for long. Instead, the pain pushed in and swamped her.

"Fine, Maverick," she whispered so that her voice wouldn't crack. "You can push me away again. But next time you feel attraction surfacing, please just leave me alone. I won't be interested."

She spun and stalked out of his room. She closed herself in her bedroom and tossed herself onto her bed before she let the tears flow silently.

It wasn't long before she heard Tanner's voice call out from the entryway below. But she didn't get up, didn't want to see him, and most certainly didn't want to say goodbye to Maverick.

When, a short while later, the heavy steps and thump of a cane told her that Tanner was helping Maverick leave, she swiped at her cheeks and held her breath as he drew near her door.

She wanted him to stop and tell her that he'd been wrong, that he needed to be with her. But his footsteps didn't hesitate as he shuffled past. Instead, he was soon descending the stairs and in the front hallway and then out the door.

A few minutes later, the wagon wheels began to rumble down the lane away from the house. Only then did she bury her face in her pillow and let the sobs come.

The relationship that had started to bloom between her and Maverick was over before it'd had a chance to grow. Now it never would. Not after he'd trampled it into the ground right alongside her heart.

19

The knocking on Hazel's bedroom door was persistent, rousing her from her melancholy.

"It's me, Sterling," a muffled voice said from the hallway.

"I'm not feeling well." She responded with the answer she'd been giving to everyone who'd come to check on her.

She'd been miserable since Maverick left two days ago. That day she'd tried to keep herself busy with chores and helping with the livestock. By the next morning, however, she'd been too distraught and hadn't gotten out of bed. This morning she'd done the same and stayed under her covers.

Mother and Scarlet had been doting on her, even though she'd assured them they had nothing to worry about, that her ailment wasn't serious. Jo-Jo had been in and out of the room too, trying to get her eating and drinking.

But Hazel didn't have an appetite, and all she wanted to do was sleep—and forget about Maverick.

"Can I come in?" Sterling asked through the door.

"No, not right now." She wasn't in the mood to see anyone, much less Sterling. He was always perceptive and would see that her sickness had more to do with her inner turmoil than a physical condition.

She pressed a hand against her nightgown and her chest to the empty cavity deep inside. She'd never known that rejection could rip her apart so thoroughly and leave her so devastated. Or maybe she'd felt everything so keenly because it was Maverick, and she loved him more than anything or anyone else in her life.

Tears stung her eyes, but instead of shedding them again, she blinked them back. She'd already cried enough over Maverick, and he didn't deserve any more of her tears.

With the silence outside the door, she released a tight breath.

"I'm coming in, Hazel." Sterling's voice contained a finality that brooked no arguments.

As the door opened, she shifted so that she was facing away from him.

It was past dusk, and he'd likely returned home for the evening meal and learned from Mother or Scarlet that she hadn't been out of bed all day. Now he was coming to scold her to get up and be productive. Or maybe he'd figured out she was in bed because of Maverick's departure. She wouldn't put it past Sterling to have seen her attraction toward Maverick and realized her melancholy had to do with his leaving.

Whatever the case, she didn't want to talk to Sterling. She wanted to be left alone to sleep—the only place she could find respite from the pain of Maverick's rejection.

The door clicked closed, and Sterling's heavy steps crossed to the bed. He stood at her bedside for several moments before a shuffling and scraping indicated that he'd lowered himself into the bedside chair. Hopefully that didn't mean he was planning to stay for a while. If so, she'd have to pretend to fall asleep.

"Hazel?" His voice was gentle.

She pinched her eyes closed.

After several long seconds, he blew out a breath. "Tell me what's wrong."

"I'm just tired and weak."

"Since when are you too tired and weak to go to work?"

A lump rose in her throat. Even after Sterling's failed wedding, she'd only missed one day of work. And yes, she'd missed going during the couple of days Maverick had been her patient. But beyond that, she'd never willingly stayed away.

"What's going on, Hazel?"

"I told you—"

"No. Tell me the truth." His voice was low and demanding.

"You wouldn't understand." How could he? Not when she didn't even really understand everything. Besides, there was no sense admitting she liked Maverick when it didn't matter anymore. She was keeping her resolve—she didn't want to be with someone who could leave her so easily, who wasn't willing to fight for her.

"Does this have to do with Maverick?" Sterling's question ended with a growl.

What did Sterling know about her and Maverick? Had he sensed their attraction?

She rolled over to find Sterling watching her with a furrowed brow.

"Did he do something?" Sterling's tone was menacing, as if one misstep from Maverick would put a rift back into their relationship.

She couldn't say anything, didn't want to be the cause of their relationship deteriorating again. Not after they'd just started repairing it.

"What did he do?" Sterling sat up straight and cracked the knuckles of first one hand and then the other.

"He didn't do anything." And that was the trouble. He hadn't been ready to do anything to try to make their relationship work.

As if hearing the despair in her tone, Sterling grew motionless. His dark-brown eyes turned murky. "You're upset because Maverick didn't do anything?"

She didn't respond. But she also didn't turn away from Sterling this time.

He studied her face, and his expression began to soften. Could he see what she wasn't willing to put into words?

"I should have seen it earlier," he finally said quietly.

"Seen what?"

"That you're in love with Maverick."

Swift tears filled her eyes.

"When?" Sterling's question was void of anger. In fact, he seemed resigned, which was more than she'd expected.

What did it matter now if she told him the truth? "I think I've always loved him."

"Always?"

"Yes, always." Maybe even from the first moment she'd met him, when his family had ridden over to welcome them to Summit County and he'd bounded over to her, lanky and handsome even when he was thirteen and she was only nine.

Sterling cracked his knuckles again. "We promised each other that we wouldn't ever let ourselves develop feelings for each other's sisters."

"You did?"

Sterling nodded solemnly.

She could see the storm cloud forming inside him and guessed he felt betrayed by Maverick. Again. "No, it wasn't like that. Maverick never noticed me. I've always just been his best friend's little sister."

Hanging his head, Sterling leaned forward, his elbows on his knees.

"I vow it, Sterling. Maverick never showed any interest in me beyond friendship."

With his head bowed low, Sterling clasped his hands together.

"You have to believe me."

"I do," he whispered.

She released a breath she hadn't known she was holding.

"I've always known he liked you," Sterling continued. "Maybe that's why I had him make the pact with me."

"He doesn't like me." She couldn't hold back the bitterness that crept into her tone.

Sterling twisted his thumbs around each other, almost nervously. "Actually, last week he told me he loves you."

Her heart stopped beating, and a strange silence settled through the brokenness of her chest. Maverick had told Sterling he loved her? Before he'd said it to her?

She wanted to push Sterling to say more, to tell her everything. But she knew her brother wouldn't say anything he didn't want to.

Sterling cleared his throat. "He rode over the day after the big snowstorm stranded you at the Oakleys'."

The morning after their kiss? Where had she been? Had she been home, or had she still been at High C Ranch?

"He told me that he slept with you and kissed you."

Heat flooded her cheeks. "It wasn't like that. It was innocent—"

"I know."

"It didn't mean anything."

"It meant something to him, because he came over with every intention of asking for my permission to court you."

"He did?" Hope sparked to life inside her, but just as quickly she doused it. It didn't matter. Maverick had walked away from her, and that was the end of them.

"I told him to stay away from you."

She pushed up, her loose hair tumbling about her in disarray. Now Maverick's distance that week after their first kiss made more sense. When Sterling had shut him down, he'd tried to honor Sterling's request to stay away from her.

Sterling still hung his head. "I'm guessing that's why he left our ranch and went home."

"Why?"

"Because he's still trying to keep his word."

Maybe that second kiss a few days ago had scared

him, made him realize how difficult it would be to resist being together. Maybe that was also why he'd refused to let her live at High C Ranch and take care of him. He wanted to do the right thing and honor his friendship with Sterling.

She could respect Maverick's integrity and his desire to remain true to Sterling. But what about her? What about what she wanted? Did it matter to him at all? At the very least, he could have discussed the situation with her and shared his conflict. Maybe they could have gone to Sterling together and tried to talk sense into him.

But Maverick had made up his mind that his friendship with Sterling was more important than her. And he'd left her without a single look back.

"This is all my fault, Hazel." Sterling sat up and met her gaze, his eyes filled with regret. "I never should have told Maverick to stay away from you. It was unfair to both of you."

"It doesn't matter now."

"Yes, it matters." Sterling clambered to his feet and combed his fingers through his messy hair. "I'm going over to see Maverick tonight and make the matter right."

"You can't."

"It's the least I can do." He started toward the door.

Panic bubbled up inside—a panic she didn't understand, except that she knew she couldn't let Sterling ride over to the High C Ranch and talk to Maverick.

"No." She shoved off the covers, ready to jump out of bed and physically stop Sterling if she had to. "Please, Sterling."

He halted, one hand on the doorknob.

Had he heard the desperate plea in her tone? "I don't want to be with a man who chooses his best friend over me."

Sterling didn't move, didn't even turn around.

"I want a man who wants to be with me so badly he'll defy everyone and everything so that he can have me. And clearly that's not Maverick."

Sterling shifted enough that she could see the haggardness in his handsome features. "I'll talk to Mav, and he'll see reason."

"Please don't." The panic was still roiling through her stomach. "I especially don't want a man who will only pursue me when he gets permission."

"It's more complicated than that. With everything that happened at the wedding, he was just trying to repair our friendship."

She slipped off the bed, ready to tie Sterling up and hold him back if he persisted. "I've already made up my mind. I don't want Maverick any longer."

"Fine." His shoulders slumped in defeat. "I won't go. At least, not today."

She dropped back to the bed, her legs suddenly weak. If only she could take away her desire for Maverick. But the truth was, she would probably always want him. The only thing she could do was stay away from him until she could convince her heart that he wasn't the right man for her.

20

Hazel hadn't come to work again.

From the way the sun was slanting through the high, open barn window, Maverick could tell that midmorning had come and gone. And that meant another day would pass without being near her. A total of six days.

He couldn't remember ever going so long without seeing her in all the years he'd known her. And the plain truth was that he wasn't sure he could make it through another day, maybe not even another hour, without her.

He gave Candy a final pat, then backed out of the stall and latched the gate behind the mare and foal. Even though he tired easily and still had to use the cane for balance, he'd pushed himself hard and was walking and riding again—at least short distances.

Even so, during the past week, he'd been restless and unable to focus long on anything. Especially yesterday and today. He hadn't been able to eat or sleep or work well. He hadn't even been able to think about much else except Hazel—wondering how she was getting along and what she was doing now that she wasn't working with the mares.

She'd rarely skipped work over the years. Now to miss all week? He must have hurt her more than he'd realized when he left her.

He'd thought he was being noble by putting space between them and preventing temptation. He hadn't wanted to keep kissing her and spending time with her and getting closer. Especially not after finally making things right with Sterling.

Sterling had not only rescued him from the river embankment but also brought him back to his house, placed him in his bed, and helped him through the first couple of rough days of recovery. In addition, he'd humbly apologized for how he'd reacted at the wedding and for so easily pushing aside their friendship.

With Sterling willing to be friends again, Maverick hadn't wanted to jeopardize that in any way, including going back on his word to stay far away from Hazel. Except that every time Hazel had entered the bedroom, his attraction to her had flared so that he'd felt like he'd combust if he stayed another day with her sitting beside his bed when all he wanted to do was pull her into the bed with him.

His thoughts had been running away from him so

wildly that he'd finally made plans with Tanner to go home. And it was a good thing he had, because the last morning, when she'd walked into his room all beautiful and fresh and like sunshine, he'd been tempted again to pull her down onto the bed and kiss her until they were both breathless.

He hadn't expected Hazel to care quite so much that he was returning home or to insist on coming with him. He'd thought they'd go back to their relationship the way it had always been—being friends and coworkers. At least, until his friendship with Sterling was solid and he was able to have another conversation with his friend.

But her words from that morning echoed in his head again as they had all week. *I thought we were starting to care about each other. I thought you wanted to be with me . . . like I want to be with you.*

She'd wanted to be with him.

Her words had tugged at the desire within him then and did so again now.

With each passing day, all the reasons for leaving her seemed flimsier, and he was beginning to realize how rash he'd been, how impetuous, how foolhardy. Once again.

With a sigh, he twirled a piece of straw between his teeth. He should have talked to her more, maybe tried to explain how he was feeling, even if it was embarrassing to admit how much he craved her. And he should have figured out a way to tell her about Sterling's ultimatum without causing angst between the brother and sister.

Now, instead of things returning to normal, maybe he'd ruined things between himself and Hazel, and he didn't know how he could keep on going without trying to repair their relationship.

He tossed the straw to the ground and started toward the exit with his cane thumping in the hay. He had to ride over to the Noble Ranch today. He wasn't gonna do anything else until he saw her and made sure she was all right.

With uneven steps, he made it halfway across the haymow before he stopped. What was he thinking? He couldn't go. He slapped a hand to his forehead then pivoted and stalked back the way he'd come.

Her last words came rushing back to him: *You can push me away again. But next time you feel attraction surfacing, please just leave me alone. I won't be interested.*

She wanted him to leave her alone. She wasn't gonna be interested in him anymore. And she was making that mighty clear with her absence.

"Maverick?" Clarabelle paused in grooming the mare in the stall across from him. With the gate open, she stood beside a chestnut Morgan, her brush suspended, her wide green eyes upon him.

His sisters had been helping in the mare barn during Hazel's absence. But it had been a strain on both of them with all their other responsibilities, especially since Ma's care continued to grow more demanding.

Clarabelle's face was shadowed with dark circles under her eyes, and she bit back a yawn. "With all the pacing and muttering, you look like you're going mad."

"I am going mad." He limped back the way he'd come, his steps slower than usual. But he was thankful he was walking at all and that the pain from the pinched nerve wasn't as debilitating when he was up as it was when he was resting.

"Because you miss the woman you love?" Clarabelle's comment was tentative. The more naturally reserved of his sisters, Clarabelle didn't often speak her mind.

But it was clear Clarabelle had figured out how much he cared about Hazel—like Tanner had, and probably like everyone had. Maverick reckoned there was no sense in denying it. "Yep, I'm missing her something fierce." He was missing her more than fiercely, but he didn't know how else to describe the ache inside.

Clarabelle was brushing the mare again, but she smiled at him over her shoulder, her blond-red hair coiled into a fashionable knot making her look older and more mature than her nineteen years. "I don't know what you did to push her away, but it looks like you have some work to do to win her back."

"Didn't mean to push her away."

"It's obvious you did anyway."

Maverick halted again, swiped off his hat, and

jammed his fingers into his hair. He'd been a fool to walk away from Hazel. "I was just trying to keep the peace with Sterling. That's all."

Clarabelle laughed softly, as if he'd told a joke. "You're willing to give up Hazel in order to keep your friend?"

Was that what he was doing?

"If the roles had been reversed," Clarabelle continued while she groomed the mare, "Sterling would have abandoned you in a heartbeat for Violet. He wouldn't have looked back."

Even though Maverick didn't want to admit it, he knew Clarabelle was right. Because essentially, that's what Sterling had done at the wedding. He'd abandoned their friendship for Violet.

Maverick twisted at his cane, leaning on it heavily, feeling the pinch in his back. "Just because Sterling doesn't have the same loyalty to me, doesn't mean I should give up my loyalty to him."

Clarabelle met his gaze with her clear one that was full of wisdom, just like Ma's had always been. "Your friendship with Sterling is a gift, and you should keep on being a good friend to him. But the woman you love needs to take priority over anyone else. That's just the way it has to be, Mav."

Maverick swallowed a strange sense of panic that began to swell. As much as he appreciated Sterling and their long history, his loyalty had to switch to Hazel now. She was his priority, the love of his life, the only one he truly wanted.

"I've made a mess of things." He released an exasperated sigh. "Seems I'm good at that."

"We all make messes at times." With a hoof pick in hand, Clarabelle lifted one of the mare's hooves and began to dislodge mud. "Sometimes even big messes. We can walk away from them, or we can roll up our sleeves and clean them up."

Clarabelle was turning into a beautiful woman not only on the outside but inwardly too.

"Weston was always the level-headed son, and he succeeds at everything he does. If only he'd never left . . ."

"Weston has good business savvy. But Pa knew you had the heart and soul that this ranch needs."

"If Weston had been here taking care of things, Pa wouldn't have died." The statement fell out from the deep, dark recesses of the pain that he'd been trying to avoid.

Clarabelle halted and gave him her full attention, her brows furrowed. "You know that Pa always said he had no logical explanation for why he was still alive, not after all the near-death encounters he'd experienced over the years."

Maverick had heard Pa's tales over the years—the bullet that'd taken off a section of his ear in the war but missed his head; the rattlesnake bite that'd punctured the sole of his shoe but missed his heel by a fraction of an inch; the log beam that had fallen while building the house, right after he'd moved from where he would have been crushed. Pa's stories had always been entertaining.

"Pa always said he got more years than he deserved," Clarabelle said softly. "He finally reached his limit."

"But if I hadn't gone after the horse thieves that day—"

"You and Pa would have gone the next and been in just as much danger then."

Was Clarabelle right? Was he carrying the burden of Pa's death when it wasn't really his to bear?

"You and Pa were more alike than anyone else."

Maverick shook his head and started to scoff.

"Why else do you think Pa had so many dangerous adventures?" Her clear green eyes probed him. "Because he lived life to the fullest, just like you."

Tension eased from Maverick's shoulders. He wasn't sure if Clarabelle was right about everything, but it made a whole heap of sense. "How'd you get so smart?"

She tossed him another smile before picking up the next hoof. "We were blessed to grow up with parents who dedicated their lives to us. Now it's our turn to do the same to each other and our own families."

His throat closed up, and he managed a nod.

"Now go on and make things right with Hazel."

He limped again toward the barn door.

"And Mav?"

He paused and glanced back at her.

She was watching him tenderly with a big happy smile. "I love you."

"I love you too, kid."

As he finished making his way out of the barn, his heart was lighter. Even though he wasn't perfect and had made plenty of mistakes, his family still cared about him, because that's what family did for each other—they kept on loving and forgiving.

And they cared enough to speak the truth in love . . .

The plain truth was, he was always gonna make mistakes, no matter how hard he tried not to. Instead of walking away again from Hazel, he had to roll up his sleeves and clean up the mess he'd made.

He started across the yard toward the barn where they kept their work horses, his gelding among them. He could make the ride to the Noble Ranch without too much pain. At least, he hoped so. Once there, he'd talk to Sterling first. He was done asking for his friend's permission and approval. This time he'd tell Sterling his plans to court Hazel and wouldn't let any objections stop him going to Hazel next, dropping to his knees, and apologizing for leaving her.

"Maverick!" came a shout from the lane. The voice sounded an awful lot like Sterling's.

21

Maverick stumbled to a halt and turned to see Sterling riding out from the ridge of pines.

He hadn't seen Sterling since he'd left the Nobles' earlier in the week but reckoned his friend hadn't been too worried about him. Maybe Sterling had even been privately relieved to have him away from Hazel.

Maverick pulled himself up to his full height and tried not to lean on the cane, wanting to prove to Sterling that he was still a strong man and worthy of Hazel. Because now that Sterling was here, he may as well have that conversation about Hazel.

Sterling seemed in a hurry, almost jittery, as he rode across the ranch yard.

"Just the person I was coming to see," Maverick called out.

"That so?" Sterling reined in but didn't dismount. Thankfully his expression was friendly enough and the animosity was gone. It might be back soon enough, once Maverick had the chance to speak his piece. But he couldn't let the prospect of harming his friendship with Sterling stop him.

As much as Sterling meant to him, Hazel meant more. Way, way more. So much more that he couldn't live without her and had to see her as soon as possible.

Maverick squared his shoulders. "We need to talk."

Sterling's jaw was covered in the usual layer of scruff, but it was easy to see his friend clamp down hard, as though bracing himself for bad news.

"It's about Hazel."

Sterling shook his head. "Got something I need your help with first."

Maverick opened his mouth to say more about his love for Hazel, but at the sight of the determination in Sterling's eyes, he bit back his words. "What is it?"

"You up for a short ride?"

"Ain't letting anything hold me back from riding."

"That's what I figured."

Maybe he could have that conversation while on the ride. "Where to?"

"Not far."

Leave it to Sterling to be as clear as mud. "Give me a minute to saddle up."

Sterling nodded but didn't say more as Maverick hobbled away. All the while Maverick readied his mount, he tried to plan out what he would tell Sterling. Because one way or another, he was gonna say something about courting Hazel.

Soon he was following Sterling to the west into the foothills behind High C Ranch. They rode one of the trails they'd worn down when they'd been younger and more adventurous.

From behind, Maverick didn't have to hide the grimace of pain that came from every jarring movement. But that also meant he was too intent on holding back the groans to voice what he needed to about Hazel.

They hadn't gone long before Sterling started up a winding incline. It was a familiar climb—one they'd made many times over the years. At the top was a smooth stretch of hilltop that overlooked the Blue River Valley for miles both to the south and north. It was one of the best views of his family's ranch as well as the Noble Ranch.

He and Sterling had spent many a summer night there, stargazing, making plans for the future, and admiring the beauty of the land that they called home. They'd decided to call it Lover's Overlook.

Why was Sterling bringing him out to the overlook today?

"Listen, Sterling," Maverick finally said as they rounded the last switchback. "I need to talk to you about Hazel."

"She's had a bad week, Mav."

Regret slammed into Maverick with such force that his heart bottomed out. "It's all my fault."

"No, it's my fault." Sterling dug his heels into his mount to urge him up the last of the distance.

"I shouldn't have left her the way I did," Maverick called after his friend. "Fact is, as much as I respect you and our friendship, I love Hazel more. And I'm gonna start courting her."

Sterling paused, stared straight ahead, but didn't respond before he nudged his horse onto the ledge, sending a shower of rocks and dirt back down the trail.

Maverick released a groan, one containing not only his pain but his frustration. He knew convincing Sterling to let him have Hazel was gonna be hard, but he'd been hoping Sterling would find it within him to see reason.

Apparently his friend would need more convincing.

Maverick urged his horse up the final ascent. "I know you said to stay away," Maverick said as he bent low over his mount and tried to minimize the jostling as his horse climbed onto the ledge. "And believe me, I've tried. But I can't do it any longer, and I wanna be with her."

Sterling was dismounting already.

Maverick's stomach was tied full of knots, but he pushed forward with what he needed to say. "I'm sorry if you don't approve, but I can't let that hold me back any longer from the woman I love."

"Good," Sterling said over his shoulder.

Good? Maverick reined in his gelding.

Sterling knelt next to what appeared to be a blanket spread out over the grassy area. He opened a basket and began to pull items out. "Glad to hear that you're planning to cooperate. I didn't want to have to beat you up."

Maverick rubbed a hand along the back of his neck to ease the tension there.

Sterling was setting out two fine china plates and silverware.

Maverick's whirling thoughts came to a halt. What was his friend doing?

At Maverick's silence, Sterling sat back on his heels and gave Maverick his full attention, his eyes lined with sadness. "I was a terrible friend and a terrible brother."

"You were?"

"Yes. Just because I'm not able to have happiness with the woman I love—loved—doesn't mean you shouldn't have your happiness."

The conversation wasn't going at all the way Maverick had envisioned. In fact, he wasn't sure what to think. "So you're not opposed to me courting Hazel?"

"Courting her?" One of Sterling's brows cocked. "Yes, I'm opposed to courtship."

"C'mon, Sterling." Maverick's voice held frustration as well as all the passion he felt for Hazel. "Don't know when I fell in love with Hazel, but I did somewhere along the way. She's not only the most beautiful woman I know, but she's the sweetest, kindest, most amazing woman I've ever met."

"Guess she is pretty amazing if she puts up with you." Sterling's voice was serious, but his eyes had begun to crinkle at the corners as though he might smile.

Maverick didn't stop to analyze Sterling's reaction. He plunged forward with saying all that he'd rehearsed. "Hazel's my world, Sterling, and I can't live without her. I don't deserve her. She's too good for a scoundrel like me. But I'm gonna spend my life trying to be worthy of her. Reckon I'll fail at times, but when I do, I'll make it up to her every time and keep on trying to love her as best I can."

Sterling's eyes crinkled even more, and one side of his lips quirked up. "Is that all?"

"I don't need your permission to court her, but I'd sure like it." There, he'd said what he needed to and now crossed his arms.

Sterling ducked his head. Was he hiding a smile?

Maverick opened his mouth to tell Sterling to take him seriously, but before he could get the words out, he took in the arrangement of the blanket, the dishes, the goblets, and the bottle of wine.

He lifted his leg over his saddle and slid down to the ground gingerly, bracing himself with his cane. Was this what he thought it was?

When his gaze drifted back to Sterling, this time his friend was wearing a wide grin. "Did I get all the details the way you wanted?"

Lover's Overlook was the place Maverick had always said he'd propose to his woman when he and Sterling had made their plans so long ago. Maverick hadn't wanted anything fancier than a picnic. He'd always figured the view was grand enough.

Did Sterling really expect him to propose to Hazel here today? He could admit, this was the last thing he'd expected from his friend.

"Like I said, no more courting," Sterling continued. "Even if it wasn't official courting, it was close enough, and a few years is long enough."

Sterling couldn't be serious, could he?

As if reading his thoughts, his friend held out a velvet bag with a drawstring. "You might need this."

Maverick's heart raced forward at double the speed. He took the bag from his friend, opened it, and peeked inside. "How'd you manage this?"

"Had a little help from your sisters."

Maverick replayed the conversation he'd just had with Clarabelle. Had she known what Sterling was up to? Was that why she'd been smiling when he left?

Sterling took out his pocket watch, flipped open the case, and read the time. Then he straightened and stuffed the watch back into his trouser pocket. "You and Hazel have been in love for a long time. I was just too stubborn—and maybe even jealous—to acknowledge it. And I'm sorry."

"I was too stubborn to acknowledge it too."

"Maybe you would have sooner, if not for me."

Maverick shrugged. Most likely he wouldn't have been ready before now, not mature enough to be the kind of selfless man Hazel deserved. Whatever the case, over the past few weeks, he'd finally been ready to admit his love, and now that he'd done so, he couldn't take it back. Doing so would be like trying to trap the Blue River in a bottle.

Sterling grabbed the reins of his horse. "Fact is, Maverick, Hazel adores you. She's so far gone for you I don't think she realizes any other men exist on the earth but you." His voice cracked. "You're blessed to have a woman who loves you like that."

Maverick's chest tightened with all the regrets he had for Sterling and Violet. He knew what Sterling was saying—that Violet had never felt that way about him, and he should have figured that out long before their wedding day.

"I can't—won't—stand in the way of your happiness." Sterling began to climb into his saddle.

"Thank you, Sterling." Maverick cleared his throat of the thick emotion lodging itself there. "I appreciate your blessing."

Sterling straightened himself on his mount, tipped up the brim of his hat, and then peered out over the valley below with the Noble Ranch barns small dots in the distance to the north and High C Ranch buildings closer and more distinct to the south.

He stared for a long moment, drew in a breath, then leveled his gaze on Maverick. "I'm giving you my blessing and then some."

"I appreciate that."

"I'll go get her now." Sterling shifted his horse as though to go, then stopped. "One last thing. You should know she's convinced herself that she doesn't need or want you anymore."

Even though Maverick already suspected as much, the regrets came rushing back. If only he hadn't been such a fool, so stupid, so selfish.

"Reckon I hurt her real bad by leaving her the way I did." Now it was time to clean up his mistake.

Sterling gave a solemn nod. "You'll have your work cut out for you today, my friend. It won't be easy."

"That bad?" Clarabelle's words from earlier resounded through his head. *We all make messes at times. Sometimes even big messes. We can walk away from them, or we can roll up our sleeves and clean them up.*

"She didn't want me talking to you," Sterling added.

"So she'll be mad if she finds out you were involved?"

"Hopefully, she'll eventually forgive me when she

realizes I did it out of love." Without another word, Sterling nudged his horse back toward the trail. Within seconds, he'd started his descent, disappearing from sight.

Once more, Maverick surveyed the blanket, dishes, and basket of food. One emotion filled him more than any other. Fear. Not because he was afraid to propose and get married.

He was afraid that Hazel might say no, just like Violet had to Sterling. And once Hazel said no, how would he stop himself from begging and pleading with her, just like Sterling had with Violet?

The fact was, he wasn't sure if he could accept a no from Hazel any more than Sterling had been able to accept a no from Violet.

But if he coerced her when she wasn't ready—when she harbored hard feelings toward him, when she needed more time—then she'd probably end up feeling as anxious as Violet.

After all, Hazel hadn't once told him she loved him. Course, he'd felt her interest at times. She'd kissed him back with enough passion for him to know something was there. But no doubt Violet had done the same, had maybe even had more feelings for Sterling, and look how that had turned out.

No matter what Sterling had said, maybe today wasn't the right day to propose to Hazel. Instead, he had to rein in his impetuousness and behave responsibly.

Maverick tucked the velvet bag into his trouser pocket and stuffed it deep, then he began to place the dishes back into the basket Sterling had brought up. Today he'd focus on apologizing to Hazel and rebuilding their friendship. There was no sense in rushing anything. Not if she wasn't ready.

Besides, he didn't want her to think he was proposing only because Sterling had dragged him out to do it. No, when he finally asked her to marry him, he wanted her to be certain he was doing it because it was his plan and not Sterling's.

He and Hazel had waited this long. What was a little more time?

22

Hazel trudged after Sterling, not caring where they were going.

The morning was bright, the sunshine warm, and the snow was mostly melted. The grass and shrubs were turning green, and she'd even spotted a wildflower or two.

Ordinarily, she would have been delighted by the blossoming spring, but she hadn't wanted to go anywhere or do anything. The melancholy had been so heavy that she hadn't been able to shake it all week.

Of course, that day Sterling had come into her bedroom, she'd finally gotten out of bed and started helping in the livestock barn. But her heart hadn't been in her work. All she longed for and all she thought about was Maverick—even though she tried not to.

Earlier this morning Sterling had insisted she ride with him and some of the other ranch hands to look for a few strays. She hadn't wanted to go, but he'd pestered her until she'd agreed to it.

She wasn't sure what had happened over the past week since she'd ridden Maverick's horse so bravely the day he'd been in his accident, but somehow she'd lost all her courage, and she hadn't been able to mount.

Sterling had been understanding and had asked her to go with him anyway, assuring her that they'd stick to the foothills closer to the ranch.

The hike through the rugged wilderness had only reminded her all the more of Maverick and the day they'd been looking for Candy.

Now, as she and Sterling climbed up a trail, she paused, the sadness slowing her steps. "I think I'm ready to turn back, Sterling."

Leading his mount ahead of her, he halted.

She tried to offer him a smile but knew it was weak. "I'm sorry I haven't been much help to you this morning."

He shrugged. "Thought being out here might cheer you up."

"Thank you for trying." But nothing would cheer her. Not when her life spread out so bleakly without Maverick in it. She hadn't realized until she'd been away from him how much she needed him—his grins, his charm, his teasing, his compliments. She missed their conversations, listening to his ideas and him asking for her input.

He was the nourishment for her soul, and without him, she was slowly shriveling up inside, the life ebbing from her.

Was this what it was like for Mrs. Oakley without her husband? Without his love and adoration, maybe Mrs. Oakley was shriveling up inside too.

Whatever the case, Hazel couldn't deny her need for Maverick.

Had she been too rash in stopping her work for the Oakleys? When she'd been going every day, at least she'd been able to see Maverick. That had been better than this, where he was completely cut out of her life and she had no contact with him at all.

But could she be satisfied with just seeing him and working with him and being friends without their relationship moving into anything more? She hadn't thought so the day that he'd left the Noble Ranch. She'd wanted everything with him or nothing.

But what if she had to be okay with their relationship where it was instead of pushing him for more than he was ready to give? Could she do that?

Yes, she could. She was growing desperate enough that maybe she'd keep walking right over to High C Ranch and tell Maverick that she wanted her job back. Yes, she loved her job and missed it too. But she missed him more. He meant more to her than the mares and foals and anything else.

"Will you do me a favor before we head back?" Sterling swept his gaze over the hilly terrain, his keen eyes missing nothing as he searched for the strays.

"Course."

"If you check the rest of the way up this trail, I'll check down in that ravine." He cocked his head to the nearby shrubs and the rocky slant of a slope.

She hesitated. "You'll be careful?" After Maverick's fall, she'd taken extra caution today to stay clear of any dangerous areas.

Sterling was already shifting his mount around. "I'll be fine. You be careful too."

As he passed by, she halted him with a touch to his arm. "I'm sorry for not getting back on the horse."

His eyes gentled. "I understand, Hazel. Some hurts never really heal."

Was that true of her? Would she never find healing from her fears? She'd thought she was heading in the right direction, but maybe she was too far off course to have any hope.

"I'll never heal from what happened to me either." Sterling's tone turned sad. "Won't ever love another woman as long as I live."

Hazel wanted to object, but before she could figure out what to say, he was already moving past her down the trail.

She watched his strong, proud back for a few more

seconds, a strange sadness settling inside her. Then, with a sigh, she plodded up the path.

As she rounded the last bend, she realized where she was. Lover's Overlook. The view at the top was magnificent. But more than that, she'd always known it was Maverick's proposal spot the same way the miner's cabin in Devil's Glen had been Sterling's.

She'd always thought the two were so romantic for planning out their proposals and deciding to help each other. Of course, Maverick had already helped Sterling fulfill his dream proposal that winter day back in January.

Hazel hadn't thought about the proposal spots since then, especially since Sterling's romantic plans had amounted to only hurt and heartache.

As Hazel crested the last section of the hill, she stopped short at the sight of Maverick standing in the long grass near the edge, arms crossed, peering over the valley that spread out for miles.

He wore his Stetson over his dark hair, and yet strands blew at the back of his neck. He radiated strength and purpose as he stood there, so ruggedly handsome that her breath snagged in her chest.

She'd missed seeing him—every part of him from the confident way he held himself down to his dusty trousers and scuffed boots.

His horse was grazing near the trailhead. At her presence, it lifted its head and nickered a hello.

Maverick pivoted, his blue eyes landing upon her and taking her in just as hungrily as he had that last morning together.

"Hi, angel." His soft greeting was like a caress across her body.

She almost closed her eyes at the sound of it and of his voice, but she knew she couldn't lose control of her emotions.

He didn't move except to tighten his grip on his cane.

She wanted to run to him, throw herself in his arms, and admit she was lost without him. But she forced her feet to remain where they were. "How are you doing? Are you still in a lot of pain?"

"Yep. Lots."

"I'm sorry—"

"Here." He patted his chest. "My heart hurts with missing you."

Her pulse leapt. What was he doing here on Lover's Overlook? And why didn't he look surprised to see her here? Had he and Sterling planned this encounter?

A shiver of anticipation shimmied up her backbone, making her tremble. She clutched her hands behind her back to hide the shaking.

His expression remained grave. "I was a blasted fool to leave you the way I did last week."

"It's okay—"

"It ain't okay. I shouldn't have gone. It's just that I

was having a hard time resisting you."

Oh my. If she'd still been mad at him, she wouldn't have been able to stay that way, not at his admission. "Sterling told me you visited him about us but that he told you to stay away from me."

Maverick's eyes were shadowed beneath the brim of his hat, and his face was lined with pain and weariness. "I shouldn't have listened to him. You're more important to me than anyone, even my friendship with Sterling. I was on my way over to tell you that this morning when Sterling came over and told me he was sorry for interfering in our relationship."

The pattering inside her chest tapped louder. Was Maverick apologizing and working his way toward proposing marriage? Or was she only having a wild dream?

She took a breath and tried to keep her hope from rising too high. "Sterling is a difficult man to defy. And I'm sure you didn't want to harm your friendship with him any more than it already had been."

"Instead, I harmed our friendship."

"I forgive you, Maverick."

"Don't deserve it. But thank you."

"Of course."

He peered to the mountains towering behind her, the muscles in his jaw flexing.

Was this the moment? Was he trying to formulate the

words to ask her to marry him?

She clutched her hands more tightly behind her back. She didn't want to go another day without being with Maverick. In fact, she didn't want to return to her family's ranch because it wasn't really home anymore. Home was with him, wherever he was. She'd learned that lesson well enough this past week without him.

"I'm really sorry, Hazel. Hope we can start over and that you'll give me a chance to do things right this time."

"Okay." But start over? What did that mean?

"Then you'll come back to work?" His tone held a hopeful note. "And we can go on being friends like before?"

She didn't want things to go back to the way they were before. She wanted more, so much more.

But maybe he wanted to take things slowly.

"So will you?" he asked.

Her breath caught. "Will I what?"

"Come back to work and keep being my friend?"

She could almost physically feel the letdown in her body. He wasn't proposing to her after all. He was simply repairing their relationship and asking to be friends again. If this was all he could offer, she'd have to be satisfied. The alternative of going on without him like she had the past week was unbearable. "Okay."

"You sure?"

She nodded even though the disappointment weighed heavily.

Maverick cocked his head toward the box in the grass with a blanket on top, and he gave her a ghost of a smile. "This is my proposal spot."

"I know."

"You do?" His brows lifted.

She could feel her face flush. "I heard you and Sterling talk about it when we were younger. You two were never all that secretive."

He dug one of his hands into his pocket. "Sterling thought he was making a grand gesture today by bringing us together out here, showing that he supports us and all."

Even if she'd told Sterling not to talk to Maverick, she could admit she was glad that he'd done it. At least now they knew Sterling had made up his mind to support them—whatever that might mean. And from the pace Maverick was moving, it might mean they stayed just friends for a long time.

"What do you think?" Maverick asked, watching her face.

"I think it was sweet of Sterling to go to all the trouble."

"Even if it was pushy?"

Was it pushy or was Sterling trying to give them the push they needed?

As if sensing her inner conflict, he took a step forward but then stopped. "I promise I won't propose today and rush you the way Sterling did with Violet."

"What?" Her thoughts slowed to a crawl as she tried to make sense of his statement. Did he think he was rushing her? Was that why he wasn't proposing?

"I reckon us fellas get something in our heads that we want, and then it's mighty hard to be patient for the women we love to be ready too."

Women we love. He still loved her.

Was he holding back today because he was afraid that what happened with Sterling and Violet would happen to them?

Hazel couldn't keep from furrowing her brow. What had she done to give Maverick the impression she wasn't ready?

"Listen, angel." Maverick's expression remained earnest. "I ain't gonna make the same mistake as Sterling. I'll wait for you. All right?"

The trouble was, he wasn't Sterling. She most certainly wasn't Violet. And she didn't want to wait.

She wanted Maverick today. No, in reality, she'd wanted him for years. And she didn't want to put off being with him any longer, especially since it was clear the only reason he was waiting was because of her.

She wasn't usually dramatic or forceful or even all that vocal, but today, she had to do something to prove she was serious about them. About him.

An idea began to formulate. She wasn't sure it would work, but she had to try.

23

She was still frowning.

Maverick's heart knocked hard against his chest. He was botching everything real bad. He should have stopped while he was ahead. Instead, he'd gone and asked her what she thought about Sterling's efforts to facilitate the proposal today.

He supposed on some level he'd been trying to figure out if she'd be open to it. Because there was a part of him—a really big part—that just wanted to throw caution away, get down on one knee, and ask her to marry him.

But look where throwing caution away had gotten Sterling—jilted on his wedding day.

"Let's forget about this." He waved his hand to the box and blanket.

She seemed to be wavering, almost as if she wasn't sure she even wanted to come work for him again.

"Please, Hazel?" He didn't care that he was pleading.

She finally nodded. "Will you do one thing for me first?"

He'd do literally anything for her. But he reined back his emotions and nodded. "Course I will, angel."

She glanced warily at his horse. "Ride with me into town?"

During those couple of days when she'd tended him after his accident, they'd talked about how she'd had no choice but to get on his horse and go for help. Even though he'd been proud of her for overcoming her fear, he reckoned she was gonna have battles to face in learning to get on a horse again. So now, with her suggestion to ride into town, he arched his brow. "You aiming to mount my horse?"

She took the reins and then brushed her hand across the gelding's forelock. "There's something really important I have to do. So I guess I don't have much of a choice."

He started to cross to her. He loved the way the sunlight streamed across her hair in a long braid, making it the finest, prettiest blond he'd ever seen. And he loved the way her cheeks were rosy, her eyes bright, and her lips set with determination.

As he reached her side, his body physically ached with the need to touch her, but he gripped his cane to keep himself from being too bold and possibly scaring her away.

She stroked the gelding another moment before more furrows appeared on her pretty forehead. "Maybe I should wait. You probably shouldn't ride that far today anyway."

"Ain't that far to town." It might cause him some pain, but it would be worth it if he could help her take one more step in facing her fear of being on a horse.

"Are you sure?" She dropped the reins. "Never mind, it was a bad idea."

"Naw." He stuck a foot in the stirrup and hoisted himself into the saddle. Even though every move was painful, he grinned and reached down a hand for her. "Let's go."

She peered up at him, her eyes wide and filled with uncertainty.

"We'll go into town, and then when you're done, we'll head back to the ranch, and you can predict how many days until Blackberry has her foal."

Her eyes narrowed for just an instant with what he could only describe as protest. But then she stuck her foot in the stirrup and grabbed hold of the pommel.

He scooted back to make room for her in front of him.

As she swung up and settled into the tight space, her proximity was almost more than he could take, with her backside tucked between his thighs, her legs touching his, and her arms and elbows bumping him.

Every curvy, beautiful part of her was there for the

taking. In fact, she probably wouldn't mind if he slipped his hand onto her waist to steady and hold her for the duration of the ride. He could lean against her as he gripped the reins and guided the horse. Or maybe he could even wrap one arm around her entirely.

But he held the reins with one hand and settled the other on his thigh. He couldn't touch her now, because if he did, he wasn't sure he'd be able to stop. He'd probably end up bending in and brushing a kiss against that long, delicate stretch of her neck that was so close and practically made for him to kiss.

He swallowed hard and looked away. "Ready?" His voice came out tight, almost curt.

"I think so." She shivered. Or maybe she was shaking from fear.

He gave himself a mental slap. He was being selfish. Now wasn't the time to be thinking about how much he desired her. He had to be looking out for her and how difficult this ride would be for her.

"Hey." He spoke as gently as he could. "I'm here. You're gonna be okay."

She drew in a breath—or tried to—and then nodded.

As they started down the trail, he kept the gait even and slow for both of their sakes. At the bottom of the winding path, they caught sight of Sterling driving a stray calf from a spot of brush. He paused a moment and homed in on Hazel's finger, likely looking to see if she was wearing an engagement ring.

His questioning eyes lifted to Maverick's, as if to ask what had happened.

Maverick shook his head and tried to give Sterling what he hoped was a look of reassurance that everything was okay. Maybe their proposals hadn't gone the way either one of them had planned, but those plans had been made by young men who hadn't known the complications of love and relationships.

All that really mattered was that Hazel had forgiven him and was willing to come back to the ranch and work. He couldn't ask for more than that right now. Instead, over time, he'd win her heart and earn her love. While he didn't want to take too long, he was also willing to wait forever to be with her.

When Hazel called out that they were riding into town, Sterling's brows rose in surprise, no doubt because Hazel was on the horse again. Thankfully, Sterling hadn't stopped them or cautioned Maverick against making the longer trip, likely because he knew how important Hazel's efforts were.

During the ride, Hazel asked him about all the mares and foals, and he spent the majority of the time updating her and answering her astute questions. The discussion distracted him from his pain to a degree, and so did her nearness. He reckoned the talk about the mares had helped take her mind off her fears too.

But by the time Breckenridge came into view, his body ached from not only his injuries but also holding himself back from her. When he finally reined in the horse and she slid down, he couldn't contain a soft groan.

She peered up at him, concern etching a line between her brows. "That was too far, wasn't it?"

"I'm fine, angel." He arched his aching back and then swung out of the saddle.

The town at midmorning was busy with mostly miners and businessmen milling about. A few teamsters were loading up for the return trip over Boreas Pass to Denver. Other wagons were readying to leave for the gold and silver mines farther into the mountains.

With the newly discovered silver veins—including Hazel's father's—the town was growing too rapidly to keep up. There were canvas tents around the edges of town, but clapboard businesses with their false fronts were in the majority now, taking the place of most log structures that had existed when his family had moved into the area. In addition to the small, white-painted church with its tall steeple, Main Street consisted of hotels, saloons, shops, liveries, and even a seedy dance hall or two.

The hill to the east side of town was being cleared of more trees, and already Ridge Street boasted of a bank, assay office, and newspaper office, and more buildings were being constructed with every passing week.

Hazel hadn't taken her concerned gaze from him. "I shouldn't have brought you here."

"You want me to be honest?" He steadied himself against his horse.

"Yes. Always."

He leaned in near her ear so that no one passing by would hear his comment. "Having you so close that whole ride and not being able to touch you is what's caused me the most pain."

She pulled back, her eyes widening and a flush coloring her cheeks.

He flashed her what he hoped was his most charming smile. He might not have proposed to her today, but that didn't mean he was holding back on using his wiles to win her.

She ducked her head, but not before he saw the beginning of a smile.

He drew in a breath, letting himself hope that she'd fall for him sooner rather than later. "So, what's your business in town?"

She peeked at him sideways, her gaze suddenly shy. "I need to speak to someone."

In the middle of looping the lead line around a hitching post, jealousy sliced through Maverick. "Who?"

She didn't answer him. Instead, she glanced both ways up and down Main Street and then darted across the road, dodging a mud puddle along with a wagon lumbering past. When she was across, she turned and smiled at him.

At the sight of her standing there, so beautiful with her tender smile beckoning to him and her bronze eyes filled with warmth, his chest swelled with all the love and desire that had been building for years.

He loved her and wanted to shout it so all the town could hear him, so that every man for miles around would know that she belonged to him. He took a deep breath and almost gave in to the need, but he forced it down and made himself go slow—just the way he'd warned himself out on the overlook.

"Wait for me," she called. "I'll be right out."

Before he could answer, she hurried up the few wooden steps to the church door. She opened it, stepped inside, and then closed the door behind her.

He finished securing his horse, then meandered across the street, studying the simple structure that had been built last summer with his pa overseeing the project. He and his pa and his brothers had worked hard to construct the chapel with a little office attached so that Reverend Livingston, a new young fellow with a nice wife and baby, would have a real church to work out of instead of one of the hotel dining rooms.

The reverend had made it widely known that the church would always be unlocked and that he'd be in his office most mornings, available for anyone who needed him, even if just for a listening ear. In the afternoons, the reverend could be seen riding around town and the surrounding areas, visiting with parishioners and others who needed help.

Reverend Livingston was a caring and godly man, and they were blessed to have him in their community. The question was, why did Hazel need to talk to him today?

Maverick leaned against the step rail, taking some of the pressure off his legs. It was the same railing he'd nailed in right beside his pa. Maverick could almost see his pa kneeling in the dry tufts of grass beside the building, looking up at him.

His pa's smile had been happy that day, even proud, because he'd had all his boys working with him doing something worthwhile. He'd stood and clamped Maverick on the shoulder and teased him. "Reckon I needed to get this church built so that maybe you'll think about finally getting married in it to your gal."

At the time, Maverick had laughed off the teasing about getting married to Hazel in a church or elsewhere. He'd insisted then, as always, that Hazel was his friend and nothing more.

But now, Maverick peered up into the cloudless sky. "Reckon you knew I loved her, didn't you, Pa?"

Maverick waited—not for an answer, but for the sadness and guilt that came so often whenever he thought about Pa. But strangely, a feeling of acceptance wafted through him. Acceptance that his pa was gone? Or maybe even acceptance that he wasn't perfect and didn't have to be?

Although the past months hadn't been easy, maybe in learning to ask for forgiveness and make amends, he'd finally begun to find peace.

The church door swung open, and Hazel smiled at him shyly. She'd discarded her duster coat and stood in her simple blouse and corduroy skirt, almost as if she planned to stay. Her cheeks were rosier than before, and she'd unplaited her hair so that now it hung down in long thick waves, nearly to her waist.

His breath got lost somewhere inside him and so did his voice. He could only stare at her like a bumbling idiot.

"Ready?" She held out a hand to him.

He didn't know what he was expected to be ready for, but he took her hand anyway. He couldn't have resisted her even if he'd tried. She could have been leading him to his execution and he would have gone with her.

She tugged him up the last of the stairs and into the chapel, closing the door behind them. She didn't release his hand but instead situated hers more securely within his, intertwining their fingers intimately.

He looked down at their hands, speechless again. When he searched her face to try to make sense of her sweet interaction, she nibbled at her lip. "Is this okay?" she whispered with a nod down the aisle.

There, at the front of the chapel, stood Reverend Livingston along with Mr. Dewitt, the hotel owner from next door, who appeared disheveled and breathless, as if he'd just been dragged into the church—and sure enough, the side door was wide open.

The reverend and Mr. Dewitt were both grinning broadly, the reverend in his suit looking especially short and thin next to the large-boned hotel owner, like a young steer next to a strapping ox.

Hazel began to move down the aisle.

Maverick was loath to let go of her hand and kept in step with her. He reckoned that now that he had hold of her hand, he probably wouldn't let go of it ever again—or at least, not for a long while.

Mr. Dewitt was smoothing back his scraggly hair and at the same time trying to tuck in his flannel shirt. "If I'd known you needed a witness, Reverend, I would have changed into something nicer."

"You're fine just the way you are," the reverend said in his soft-spoken tone. "This won't last long." He was flipping open what appeared to be his prayer book.

Were they having a service of some sort? What exactly was going on?

With only a dozen or so wooden pews on either side of the aisle, the walk to the altar was over before Maverick could make sense of what was happening, and he found himself standing beside Hazel in front of the reverend and Mr. Dewitt.

Hazel gazed at the reverend as if waiting for him to begin the service.

Maverick lifted his brows at her in question, but she kept her focus ahead.

Reverend Livingston made the sign of the cross, then began to read from the book in front of him. "Dearly beloved, we are gathered together here in the sight of God and in the face of . . . this witness, to join together this man and this woman in holy matrimony, which is an honorable estate instituted of God—"

"Wait, what?" Maverick blurted.

"It's. Instituted. Of. God." Mr. Dewitt enunciated each word.

"I realize that—"

"Hush now, Maverick." Hazel's hand in his tightened. "You're interrupting our marriage ceremony."

A strange, excited tremor flowed through him. "We're getting married?"

She peeked at him sideways. "I know you said you'd wait, but I don't want to wait."

The trembling in his core trailed to his limbs, so that he was suddenly weak. "You don't want to wait?"

"No. I've waited long enough to be with you."

Was this really happening to him?

He glanced to the reverend and Mr. Dewitt, who were now watching him with wide eyes, clearly as unprepared for this twist in the ceremony as he was.

Hazel turned so that this time she was facing him squarely. Her expression was more serious than he'd ever seen it before, and she lifted her chin almost defiantly. "I want to marry you today. Now. And I never want to be away from you ever again."

He was usually the impetuous one, but he'd tried earlier to be cautious and go slow and be responsible. Now Hazel was turning everything upside down.

She clutched his hand and tugged him closer. "I love you, Maverick."

He couldn't formulate a response. All he could do was pull her into his arms and lower his lips to hers. There was no gentle start. No, he couldn't restrain himself any longer. His kiss was hard and hungry, filled with all the wanting that words couldn't express.

Her kiss in return was almost desperate, as if she was afraid he wouldn't accept what she was offering. Surely she had to know he would have taken whatever she'd been willing to give him, even if it had been only crumbs. And surely she had to know that if she was offering him everything, he was gonna take it without a single question.

But just in case she had any doubt, he broke the kiss and nuzzled her neck. "You're the love of my life and the only thing I'm living for, angel."

Just to make sure she understood how much he loved her, he touched his lips to hers, this time softly but with enough promise to let her know that the kiss was just the beginning of many more.

The reverend was smiling and looking at his prayer book, and Mr. Dewitt was whistling under his breath and staring at the ceiling. "Guess I know who will be using my best room when this is over."

Hazel's lashes fell against her flushed cheeks.

Maverick grinned at the idea of using Mr. Dewitt's best room for a day or two or three. That was definitely gonna happen. But first . . .

Maverick released her hand, dug in his pocket, then pulled out the velvet bag. He opened the drawstring and slid out a ring. It was a gold band, delicate like Hazel and yet so strong.

Maybe she would have accepted it today if he'd proposed to her on Lover's Overlook, but he liked how this had worked out. It had happened in a way he never could have planned even if he'd tried.

He held the ring up. "I've been ready to marry you for a long time too. No more waiting."

"Does this mean you're done interrupting, and we can finish the ceremony?" Hazel smiled, and the beauty of it went straight to his heart.

He slipped the ring on her finger. "It means I can't think of anything I'd like to do more." And he meant it.

24

The final shovel of dirt landed in place over the coffin.

Hazel held Maverick's hand tighter and rested her head against his arm, hoping he could feel her comfort.

His body was hard and stiff and unyielding as he stood beside the rest of his family at the graveside of their mother. His body had been hard and stiff and unyielding ever since the dear woman had passed two days ago.

Hazel knew Maverick blamed himself for his ma's deterioration over the months after his pa's passing, but he wasn't to blame for his ma's death any more than his pa's. The good thing was that Maverick had finally made peace with his pa's passing, and she knew that over time he'd do the same thing with his ma's.

Sterling rested his shovel in the long grass and stepped back to stand with Mother, Father, Scarlet, and other friends of the Oakleys who had come to the funeral to support the family.

Maverick's siblings were all there. Weston stood beside him—had ridden up from Fairplay yesterday with his wife Serena and their little boy.

Ryder hunched beside Weston, his head down, his grief more palpable than anyone else's. It was almost like a mountain lion pacing back and forth. His wife hadn't come with him. If the rumors were true, she'd run off and was now living with another fellow even though she was expecting Ryder's baby.

Tanner was between Clarabelle and Clementine, his head down too. He'd been off in the wilderness like always, and they hadn't been sure if word of the death would reach him in time for the funeral. But somehow he'd gotten the message and had traveled all night and arrived at the cemetery just in time.

Clarabelle and Clementine had taken the death hard too, blaming themselves the same way Maverick was. They'd cried lots of tears in Hazel's arms over the past two days, questioning why their ma had to go and wishing they'd done more to help her.

Reverend Livingston, at the head of the gravesite, began to pray in closing. As he did so, Hazel rubbed her thumb across Maverick's hand and prayed for him.

Her heart hurt for him, and the ache pushed up into her throat. Was it possible to love anyone more than she loved him? She didn't think so.

The beautiful memories of the past few weeks of

being married to him flashed through her mind. Those first couple of days of their idyllic honeymoon at Dewitt's Hotel. After leaving the church, Maverick had sent a message to Sterling, letting him know about the marriage and asking him to inform both of their families they'd be gone a couple of days.

When they'd finally returned to their homes, they hadn't been sure what to expect. Mostly their families had been happy with the news, although her mother had been disappointed that she hadn't been able to plan or participate in the wedding.

When they'd gone into Mrs. Oakley's bedroom, she'd only had to take one look at their faces and their locked hands to know what had happened, and she'd exclaimed that it was past time for their union. They'd spent every evening with her, hoping their visits and seeing their love for each other would revive her.

But she'd only seemed all the more content to let loose her grip of this life and move on to the next one, where she could be with her husband.

Hazel could understand to some degree Mrs. Oakley's need to be with her husband again. After being married to Maverick for three weeks, she was more intertwined with him than she'd ever believed possible. If he were ripped away from her, he'd take a part of her with him.

As the reverend's prayer came to an end, the silence around the grave was broken only by the wind whispering through the new leaves on the aspens that surrounded the cleared area of the cemetery outside of Breckenridge.

The May sunshine peeked through the clouds now and then, as if to remind them that though darkness often came, the light was always there waiting to break through, like with the miracle of the birth of another foal last night. She and Maverick had worked together most of the night for the foaling and had finally fallen asleep together in the haymow for a couple of hours.

Even with the shadows of his ma's death hanging over them, the birthing had been beautiful, and Hazel had loved that this time they hadn't needed to go their separate ways afterward, that they could hold each other and kiss in the hay to their heart's content.

As people began to mill about the gravesite, the widower Mr. Meyer, with his two young children, approached Clarabelle.

Mr. Meyer was a German immigrant with a small homestead to the east of the Oakleys. He'd lost his wife last year, and now as he watched Clarabelle interacting with his children, his eyes reflected his intentions.

Hazel knew she shouldn't eavesdrop, but as Maverick exchanged a few words with Ryder, she couldn't keep from listening as Mr. Meyer spoke with Clarabelle.

He held his hat and twisted the brim. "I am sorry for your loss, Miss Oakley."

"Thank you for coming today." Clarabelle spoke

politely back, her attention still on the children who were students at the school where Clarabelle assisted. Dieter with his fair hair was six, and Bianca had long, dark hair and was five.

"Father says you can become our new Mutti," Bianca said, "now that you're not needed at your home."

The man shook his head, his face filling with chagrin as he fired off a rebuke to his daughter in German. She said something back in German, her eyes wide and innocent.

Clarabelle retreated a step.

"I'm sorry." Mr. Meyer held out a hand as though to stop her from going. "I was not planning to ask you to marry me on a day such as this. This is not a goot day."

"It isn't a good day."

He nodded, twisting his hat even faster in his strong fingers. "I will soon a visit pay?"

Clarabelle glanced up, alarm now creasing her forehead. "I don't think I'm the right woman—"

"You will think about it, yes?" His eyes held such hope.

She hesitated.

Hazel held her breath. Of Maverick's twin sisters, Clarabelle had a harder time telling people no. But she surely wouldn't rush into a marriage decision like this, would she?

"Ready?" Maverick whispered, grasping Hazel's hand

more securely in his.

Although Hazel wanted to see how Clarabelle answered Mr. Meyer, she followed along as Maverick tugged her away from his ma's grave through the gate in the fence that surrounded the cemetery. She let him lead the way to his horse, tied up with others nearby.

Family and friends would be heading over to the High C Ranch for a feast that her mother and sister and other neighbors had prepared. Hazel would have plenty of opportunity to talk to Clarabelle later about Mr. Meyer.

For now though, at this moment, Maverick needed her. She could sense it in his every move.

He helped her up into the saddle, and though she gripped the pommel hard, her fear of riding was diminishing more and more every time she braved getting on. Of course, it helped that she always rode in front of Maverick. His presence surrounding her had a way of making her feel safe.

And of course, he liked to distract her with lingering kisses to her neck and shoulders and jaw and about any place that he could kiss from behind.

And his caresses . . .

She blushed at the thought of the bold way he touched her whenever they rode together, his hands always straying, as if he could never get enough of her.

As he mounted behind her, she relaxed against him, leaning back and relishing the feel of his hard chest and his thick arms. She could admit she was growing to like riding again just for moments like this, where their bodies were pressed against one another closely enough that she could feel his heartbeat.

He directed the horse away from the cemetery and toward the foothills, away from the main road. He was taking the long way. Even though he wasn't fully recovered from his accident, he was walking on his own without a cane and could withstand longer rides.

They rode silently, the hooves against the earth and rocks the only sound as they made their way north toward the ranch through the foothills and the rugged countryside. When finally the town was well behind them, Maverick slowed the pace until they were nearly stopped.

He released the reins and wrapped his arms around her waist, sagging into her as if he needed her more than anything or anyone.

She wrapped her arms over his and drew him nearer.

He nestled into her neck and kissed her jaw.

Warmth spiraled out from her abdomen as it did every time he kissed her, filling her with a keen need for him.

"I love you, Hazel." His voice was hoarse near her ear. "Thank you for being here for me through all of this."

She lifted her arms and wrapped them around his neck from behind, drawing him down. At the same time, she twisted so that he could reach her mouth and give her the kiss she craved.

As their lips meshed, time and space halted around them, and all that existed was the moment and their passion, his hands sliding up her ribs, hers digging into his neck, their bodies pulsing with one heartbeat and one need.

The kiss was deep, the tangling of their lips desperate, as if they both knew that life was fragile and could be taken away in a heartbeat.

He broke away, his breathing raspy against her cheek. "Let's never squander another moment that we have together."

"I won't." Her own breathing was ragged.

This man, this life they'd been given together, the love they shared. They'd waited to be together. They didn't know how long they had left. All they could do was make the most of every second of time they had together and never take it for granted.

She shifted and placed another kiss on his mouth, hard and filled with the promise of loving him forever.

Author's Note

Dear Reader,

Thank you for joining me on this adventure into the high country of Colorado! If you liked getting to know the Oakley family, then you'll be happy to hear that there will be five books in this series—one for each of the Oakley siblings. Clarabelle gets her chance at true love next. So I hope you'll look for her book, *Willing to Wed the Rancher*, and journey back to the high country for another sizzling romance!

If you missed Weston Oakley's story, then make sure you go back and read about him and his effort to find love in *Claiming the Cowgirl*. Even though it's part of my Colorado Cowgirl series, it's also a standalone, and you won't be lost if you read it without having read any of the other books. BUT you won't be disappointed if you read all the other books in the Colorado Cowgirl series too!

As always, I love hearing from YOU! If you haven't yet joined my Facebook Reader Room, what are you waiting for!? It's a great place to keep up to date on all my book releases and book news, as well as a fun place to connect with other readers and me.

Finally, the more reviews a book has, the more likely other readers are to find it. If you have a minute, please leave a rating or review. I appreciate all reviews, whether positive or negative.

Until next time . . .

I hope you fell love with Maverick and Hazel! Don't miss the next book in this sweet Western romance series, *Willing to Wed the Rancher*.

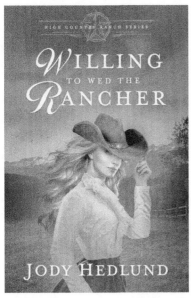

Assistant schoolteacher Clarabelle Oakley has a hard time saying no. When Eric Meyer, widowed father of two of her young students, proposes to her, she botches her effort to tell him no and that she wants to marry for love, not convenience. Only days later, the unthinkable happens, and Clarabelle learns she's been given charge of Eric's children and his farm.

Professor Franz Meyer arrives in Summit County, Colorado, to make peace with his estranged brother but discovers Eric is gone, leaving too many unanswered questions. One thing he knows for certain, however, is that he's fallen in love at first sight with Clarabelle and is determined to win her heart.

As Franz investigates what happened to his brother, danger closes in. He wants to keep Clarabelle and the children safe, but she resists the relationship because her twin sister has staked a claim on Franz. Will Clarabelle choose to say yes to love before Franz is taken from her forever?

- Twin sisters
- Love triangle
- Love at first sight
- Mystery
- Wealthy foreigner
- Fish out of water
- Estranged family

"This one's worth rounding up."—Booklist, on Falling for the Cowgirl

*All of the books in the High Country Ranch series are sweet, closed-door romances with plenty of sizzle. The inspirational themes are light, and the romance is the main focus of the books.

If you enjoyed *Waiting for the Rancher*, then check out more sweet Western romances by Jody Hedlund:

Committing to the Cowgirl

After years away, Astrid Nilsson has returned home to Colorado, hoping to become Fairplay's second doctor and to find healing for her reoccurring consumption. Dr. Logan Steele is seeking to hire a male physician to take over his clinic after he goes back East. When Astrid, his childhood sweetheart, insists that she's the one for the job, he offers her a bargain she can't refuse: pretend to court him to appease his mother and he'll give her the doctor position on a trial basis.

Cherishing the Cowgirl

Charity Courtney is at her wit's end trying to save her boardinghouse from a bank foreclosure. Wealthy railroad magnate Hudson Vanderwater hears of Charity's plight. Although he comes across as cold and callous, he is drawn to helping women in need because of a tragedy that destroyed his sister. He concocts a plan that will save Charity—he'll employ her and rent her boardinghouse for the month and in doing so alleviate her debt.

Convincing the Cowgirl

When unexpected visitors arrive at the Courtney Boardinghouse and claim the place belongs to them, Patience Courtney finds herself homeless and penniless. When wealthy rancher, Spencer Wolcott, proposes a marriage of convenience, Patience accepts the arrangement. In exchange for a new home, she agrees to become the mother to Spencer's precocious little girl so that he can manage his prosperous ranch.

Captivated by the Cowgirl

Now that her sisters are both married, Felicity Courtney manages the Courtney Boardinghouse alone. After nearly collapsing from exhaustion while caring for an invalid man and his wife who are staying at the boardinghouse, Felicity posts an advertisement for a hired hand. Philip Berg, a prince in disguise, is hiding in Fairplay while attempting to stay one step ahead of an assassin. When the spirited Felicity Courtney tacks up a notice that she is hiring help, he offers to do the job.

Claiming the Cowgirl

Serena Taylor is hiding in Colorado's high country to keep her son safe, and she knows the best way to protect him is by marrying again and giving him a father. Weston Oakley needs a wife by Christmas to placate his meddling family, but after being spurned one too many times in love, he's reluctant to give his heart away again. When they agree on a marriage of convenience, both of them get much more than they bargained for.

Keep reading for a sneak peek at *Committing to the Cowgirl*, the first Colorado Cowgirls sweet historical romance novel.

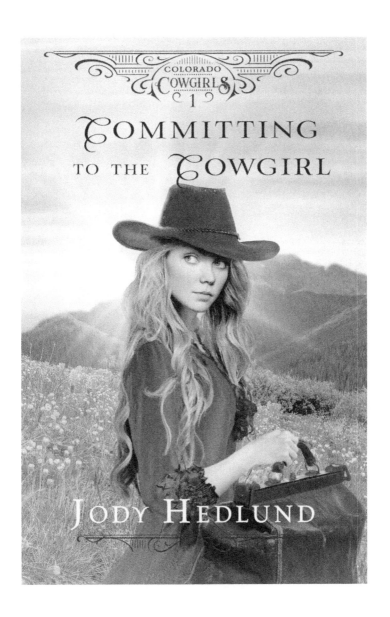

1

FAIRPLAY, COLORADO

JULY 1877

Astrid Nilsson wanted the job so badly she could taste the need for it.

She paused in front of a gray weathered building nestled among the saloons and businesses on Main Street. The words painted in bold white above the door read: *Doctor's Office*. A card in the large multi-paned window said: *Remedies, Tonics, Powders*. Another sign boasted: *Painless Tooth Extractions*.

The rugged one-story structure was smaller and more rustic than Chicago clinics. But the office was certainly better than nothing at all, which had been the case when she'd left Fairplay six years ago to begin her medical training.

She lifted a hand to knock on the rough-plank door to find that it was already open a crack.

Drawing in a breath, she straightened her black hat with its high, flat crown and narrow brim, situating the lilac and plum ribbons so they dangled behind her coiled hair but didn't disturb the light brown strands curled near her ears. She flounced the dust from the skirt of her day dress—a matching lilac and plum velvet-and-silk taffeta with an elaborate bustle at the back.

She'd already attempted to smooth out the wrinkles and grime her garments had collected during the stagecoach ride from Denver. But as she'd walked down the street from the livery, the passing wagons and horses had stirred up the perpetual dust of the high-country town and added a fresh layer to her garments—or so it seemed.

She slipped a hand into her medical bag draped over her arm and pulled out the delicate paper fan that matched her clothing. She flipped it open and flapped air over her flushed face. The high-altitude July sun was hotter than she remembered. Or maybe she'd just become accustomed to the more humid air of the Midwest.

Should she go out to her family's ranch, take a bath, rest, and apply for the position first thing tomorrow?

No. She grasped the door handle. She was doing this now. This afternoon. Before she garnered two hundred questions from her family.

Besides, she'd already resolved that whether or not she was fortunate enough to secure employment as Fairplay's second medical doctor, she didn't intend to impose on her sister Greta or any other family member. Mr. McLaughlin at the livery had informed her of a newly opened women-only boardinghouse at a homestead about a mile southwest of Fairplay. She'd take a room there.

First, she had to convince the current doctor that he needed to hire her, which would be no small feat.

She didn't have to look at the neatly clipped advertisement in her pocket. She had it memorized: *Experienced medical doctor wanted as a partner in an established practice in Fairplay, Colorado.*

Even if it hadn't ended with *No women need apply,* maybe she should have replied to the advertisement and scheduled an interview rather than showing up unannounced.

Tucking her fan back into her bag, she pushed open the door and stepped into the dim interior, the dusty front window allowing in only scant sunlight. The strong, earthy scent of camphor greeted her, as did the lingering bitterness of carbolic acid.

The front room—the size of a small parlor—was devoid of patients but contained several scuffed chairs as well as a bench, and a spittoon in the corner. The walls were painted a soothing light green, and a blue-and-green rug was positioned in the center of the floor.

A half-open door led to another room which she guessed was an examination area, one that allowed for some privacy.

Low voices came from within. Probably the doctor with a patient.

She didn't know the current physician's name. When she'd inquired of her fellow stagecoach passengers, they told her they were new to town, too, and hadn't been able to give her any information.

How many physicians had come and gone from Fairplay over the years? There had been quite a few. But a transitory nature was common in the high country, where people eventually tired of the rugged life away from civilization.

She placed her bag on the closest chair, the brown leather still shiny and the brass buckle polished to perfection. It had been a gift from Mr. and Mrs. Remington after she'd finished her medical degree at the Women's Hospital Medical College of Chicago three years ago. Unfortunately, she hadn't had many opportunities to use the bag, since most of her medical experience after graduation had been inside the Women's Hospital where a bag wasn't needed.

She'd gone on some house calls with Doctor Lawana Lewis, who had issued an invitation to assist in the practice she ran from her home south of Chicago. The apprenticeship hadn't been long or sufficient enough. But like the other female graduates, Astrid had known women physicians weren't trusted or accepted the same way men were and that the battle to find steady work would be difficult.

Expelling a sigh through her tight airways, she paced to the window and peered through the foggy layer of grime at the familiar landmarks—Simpkins General Store, Hotel Windsor, Cabinet Billiard Hall, and more. They were all there, hardly changed since the evening she'd ridden into Fairplay close to fifteen years ago when she'd been a waif of only nine. Greta had brought her to Colorado, hoping the mountain environment would cure her of consumption. And it had worked . . . for many years.

Astrid pressed a hand against her chest and pushed down a niggling tickle at the back of her throat. She hadn't told anyone about her suspicion that the consumption was returning. But she could feel her lungs filling with fluid, and her cough was getting worse.

With every passing week, she'd known she needed to return to Colorado . . . before she was too sick for any of Colorado's natural cures to work their magic again. The question was—would they work for her a second time?

She'd beaten death once. But maybe once was all she'd get. Maybe she was selfish to hope she'd have another fifteen years of life.

Regardless of whether she had fifteen months or fifteen years, she intended to make the most of her time left, and that included working for as long as she possibly could.

And it also included spending her last days close to her family . . .

Astrid stared at the general store, hoping for a glimpse of her sister coming outside, empty crates in hand after delivering her homemade jam and baked goods. The chances of the encounter were slim. It was too late in the day for Greta to be in town. And besides, nowadays Greta sold most of her products to the tourists and visitors who stayed at Healing Springs Inn.

Astrid's sights strayed to the side street past the courthouse where her friend Catherine—Mr. and Mrs. Remington's daughter—lived with her family in a lovely two-story home. Maybe she'd see the young woman milling about town with her children.

What would everyone think once they heard she was back?

She hadn't told anyone she was coming home. Of course, Mr. and Mrs. Remington could have telegrammed Catherine with the news. But that was highly unlikely since Astrid had asked them not to say anything.

Catherine had been a true friend from the moment they'd met. As a midwife, she'd been the one to encourage Astrid to pursue nurse's training. Catherine had made living arrangements with her family in Chicago. And she'd supported Astrid's decision to continue on and earn her medical degree.

Not that Greta and everyone else had opposed her change of career. They'd agreed to it. Eventually. And reluctantly. Mostly because they missed her and wanted her to live closer. Her infrequent visits home once every couple of years simply hadn't been enough, especially for Greta.

Two men's voices from the other room became more distinct, and a moment later the door of the examining room squeaked open, and chatter filled the waiting room behind her.

She shifted away from the window as a tall, slender man attired in an impeccable navy suit coat and trousers led the way to the door, his back facing her. He wasn't wearing a hat, and his neatly trimmed hair was as dark as midnight.

An older man followed him—presumably the doctor. He was much shorter, only a few inches taller than her five feet, two inches. Slightly rotund, with but a smattering of gray hair covering his head, he was attired in baggy, rumpled clothing.

He held a crumpled handkerchief and wiped at clear discharge from his purplish nose. His eyes were red and watery too. He might have catarrh. Or it was possible he was having a reaction to something in the environment. She'd recently read research that investigated the effects of hay and pollen and other airborne particles in causing rashes, itchy eyes, and wheezing.

"Champion will eventually make a fine racing horse," the younger man was saying as he opened the door.

The doctor blew noisily into the handkerchief before

stuffing it back into his pocket. "Good. Then I'll be sure to wager on him."

Despite his condition, the doctor seemed to have a kind voice and personable demeanor. She crossed her fingers that he'd be open to her joining his practice even though she was a woman. After all, a simple town like Fairplay, while it had grown over the years, didn't have much to attract a male physician.

When Mr. and Mrs. Remington had returned to Chicago several weeks ago after visiting Catherine in Fairplay, they'd brought Astrid the advertisement for the medical doctor upon Catherine's insistence. They hadn't known anything about the current doctor either, except their daughter's assurances that he was a forward-thinking man who wouldn't dismiss applicants on the basis of gender.

The doctor reached for a battered felt hat on the coat rack beside the door and situated it over his head. He stuck out his hand to his patient and exchanged a handshake, and then the doctor stepped out the door.

Unless . . .

She fixed her full attention on the younger man as he closed the door, his suit coat stretching snugly across broad shoulders and his dark hair brushing at the collar.

She'd misjudged the situation. Maybe the younger man was the doctor. Surely that was better. Such a doctor might have an open mind to a female physician more so than an older man who was set in his ways.

He began to turn away from the door. "How can I help you—?" As he took her in, he halted abruptly.

Every single function in her body halted as well at the sight of a familiar slender face with a fine nose and a square jaw that was covered in a layer of shadowy stubble. His brows rose above dark brown eyes, and his mouth hung open as though she'd rendered him speechless.

Even though she was equally taken aback, she kept her expression from giving away her surprise.

This was Logan Steele, the son of Fairplay's former mayor. Her first true love.

He'd left Colorado without a goodbye when he'd turned seventeen and she'd been sixteen. Compared to the lanky boy she'd last seen, Logan had changed. His body had filled out considerably. His face had matured. And he bore an air of assurance.

He quickly closed his mouth and let his eyes make a trail down her body before rising and widening with frank appreciation.

Did he recognize her? After the passing of the years, she'd grown up and changed a great deal too. Or maybe he was taken with her fine appearance. She was accustomed to the looks and flattery. Her blond-brown hair, silvery blue eyes, and her womanly figure along with her delicate features drew attention everywhere she went.

She'd been told by plenty of men that she was

beautiful. The trouble was, she'd grown weary of men paying attention to her outward appearance. If only they could see past her exterior to all of her other qualities that made her a good doctor. But most fellows couldn't reconcile why a pretty and fashionable woman like herself wanted to do "men's work."

Would Logan Steele be able to do so?

Even if he did see her as an equal and give her a chance to join the partnership, the real question was whether she wanted to subject herself to working with him . . . especially after the way he'd spurned her.

A part of her wanted to stomp out of the office and never look back. But the other part—the more rational, practical, controlled side—reminded her that this job was her only option. And since she wanted to practice medicine as long as she was physically able to do so, then she couldn't let a broken heart from the past keep her from doing what she loved.

Besides, the past was in the past. Logan Steele didn't mean anything to her anymore. And she'd show him that.

She lifted her shoulders and chin and gave him what she hoped was her most professional look. "I am here to inquire about your advertisement for a partner in your medical practice."

He leaned back against the wall beside the coat rack and crossed one shiny black shoe over the other before folding his arms, revealing gold-studded cuff links. The pose seemed casual, as though he had every intention of interviewing her right then and there. Except that a crooked smile tugged at his lips.

Did he think she was jesting? Some men poked fun at her when they discovered she was a doctor. It was cowardly of them to disparage her education and aspirations. But she'd learned that she'd only harm her efforts if she revealed any exasperation or anger. She had to stay calm. "You do still need another doctor to join your practice, do you not?"

"Astrid Nilsson." His lips lifted into a higher smile, one that had always been a killer. "You were the prettiest and sweetest girl in Fairplay."

Oh, please. If he'd thought she was so pretty and sweet, then why had he left her?

His gaze was back on her face, languidly taking in each detail of her features. "Looks like that's still true."

"Perhaps it is."

His dark eyes were rich and expressive, glimmering with cockiness.

Maybe she should act as though she didn't know him, at least for a few moments. She pretended to study his face. "You look vaguely familiar . . ."

"You don't remember who I am?" Logan continued to lean against the wall.

"You'll have to forgive me—"

"You were one of my first friends here in Fairplay."

His eyes leveled with hers, swallowing her so that she wanted to lose herself there, but at the same time giving her a glimpse inside to his deep, complex, and stirring soul. Those eyes had always had the power to make her breathless and weaken her knees.

Not anymore. She was stronger now. "Sorry. I can't say I remember . . . it's been so long since I've lived here . . ."

He'd always been a dashing and good-looking fellow. But somehow, he'd turned into an almost sinfully handsome man. Too handsome for anyone's good—including his own.

As though hearing the direction of her thoughts, he pushed away from the wall and started across the waiting room toward her, his eyes riveted to hers. Her heart tapped in time with his footsteps, a strange anticipation humming through her blood.

He stopped only inches away from her and towered above her petite frame by at least a foot, just like he always had. Just like the night of the barn dance the last time she'd seen him, when he'd kept cutting in on dances she was having with other fellows.

The glimmer in his eyes then had told her how much he was enjoying making the other men angry. But she hadn't minded—had been too enamored, too easily swept off her feet by the charming Logan Steele. She'd believed he was finally staking a claim on her.

After the last dance near dawn, she hadn't resisted when he'd tugged her outside. She'd been near to heaven with him holding her hand and hadn't paid attention when he'd led her around the corner of the barn, until he'd tugged her close and dropped a kiss on her lips—her first kiss. Even though the kiss had been short and sweet, it had sent her to the moon—no, it had sent her to the stars.

Of course, if she'd been thinking straight, she would have realized much sooner that Logan hadn't been serious. Because after the kiss, he'd spun, walked away, and ridden out of her life.

Several days later, she'd learned that he'd left for the East—without a word, without a goodbye, without a glance back. After their years of friendship and after what she'd assumed was a mutual attraction, she'd been stunned and devastated.

She hadn't seen him since.

During her rare visits home, she'd heard tales of his adventures from Landry Steele and his wife, who liked to talk about their only son who was doing such great things in the East, becoming one of Boston's best physicians. But as far as Astrid was concerned, the moment Logan had left her at the dance, he'd written himself out of her life. And she intended to keep it that way.

"It's Logan Steele, Astrid. How can you forget about me?"

"Oh, w-e-l-l, Logan Steele. Clearly you think more highly of yourself than you ought to."

"I thought we got along rather well as friends. In fact, I'd say we ended up more than that."

Yes, she'd given him her heart, then he'd walked away without any explanation at all.

A long-buried spark of anger flared to life. Before she could rationalize or make sense of what she was doing, she lifted her hand and slapped his cheek.

Get your copy of Committing to the Cowgirl now!

Jody Hedlund is the bestselling author of more than fifty novels and is the winner of numerous awards. Jody lives in Michigan with her husband, busy family, and five spoiled cats. She writes sweet historical romances with plenty of sizzle.

A complete list of my novels can be found at jodyhedlund.com.

Would you like to know when my next book is available? You can sign up for my newsletter, become my friend on Goodreads, like me on Facebook, or follow me on Instagram.

Newsletter: jodyhedlund.com

Facebook: AuthorJodyHedlund

Instagram: @JodyHedlund

Made in the USA
Las Vegas, NV
07 October 2024

96381372R00173